The Celestial Omnibus ar

E. M. Forster

The Story of a Panic

I.

Eustace's career – if career it can be called – certainly dates from that afternoon in the chestnut woods above Ravello. I confess at once that I am a plain, simple man, with no pretensions to literary style. Still, I do flatter myself that I can tell a story without exaggerating, and I have therefore decided to give an unbiased account of the extraordinary events of eight years ago.

Ravello is a delightful place with a delightful little hotel in which we met some charming people. There were the two Miss Robinsons, who had been there for six weeks with Eustace, their nephew, then a boy of about fourteen. Mr. Sandbach had also been there some time. He had held a curacy in the north of England, which he had been compelled to resign on account of ill-health, and while he was recruiting at Ravello he had taken in hand Eustace's education – which was then sadly deficient – and was endeavoring to fit him for one of our great public schools. Then there was Mr. Leyland, a would-be artist, and, finally, there was the nice landlady, Signora Scafetti, and the nice English-speaking waiter, Emmanuele – though at the time of which I am speaking Emmanuele was away, visiting a sick father.

To this little circle, I, my wife, and my two daughters made, I venture to think, a not unwelcome addition. But though I liked most of the company well enough, there were two of them to whom I did not take at all. They were the artist, Leyland, and the Miss Robinsons' nephew, Eustace.

Leyland was simply conceited and odious, and, as those qualities will be amply illustrated in my narrative, I need not enlarge upon them here. But Eustace was something besides: he was indescribably repellent.

I am fond of boys as a rule, and was quite disposed to be friendly. I and my daughters offered to take him out – 'No, walking was such a fag.' Then I asked him to come and bathe – 'No, he could not swim.'

"Every English boy should be able to swim," I said, "I will teach you myself."

"There, Eustace dear," said Miss Robinson; "here is a chance for you."

But he said he was afraid of the water! – a boy afraid! – and of course I said no more.

I would not have minded so much if he had been a really studious boy, but he neither played hard nor worked hard. His favorite occupations were lounging on the terrace in an easy chair and loafing along the high road, with his feet shuffling up the dust and his shoulders stooping forward. Naturally enough, his features were pale, his chest contracted, and his muscles undeveloped. His aunts thought him delicate; what he really needed was discipline.

That memorable day we all arranged to go for a picnic up in the chestnut woods – all, that is, except Janet, who stopped behind to finish her watercolor of the Cathedral – not a very successful attempt, I am afraid.

I wander off into these irrelevant details, because in my mind I cannot separate them from an account of the day; and it is the same with the conversation during the picnic: all is imprinted on my brain together. After a couple of hours' ascent, we left the donkeys that had carried the Miss Robinsons and my wife, and all proceeded on foot to the head of the valley – Vallone Fontana Caroso is its proper name, I find.

I have visited a good deal of fine scenery before and since, but have found little that has pleased me more. The valley ended in a vast hollow, shaped like a cup, into which radiated ravines from the precipitous hills around. Both the valley and the ravines and the ribs of hill that divided the ravines were covered with leafy chestnut, so that the general appearance was that of a many-fingered green hand, palm upwards, which was clutching convulsively to keep us in its grasp. Far down the valley we could see Ravello and the sea, but that was the only sign of another world.

"Oh, what a perfectly lovely place," said my daughter Rose. "What a picture it would make!"

"Yes," said Mr. Sandbach. "Many a famous European gallery would be proud to have a landscape a tithe as beautiful as this upon its walls."

"On the contrary," said Leyland, "it would make a very poor picture. Indeed, it is not paintable at all."

"And why is that?" said Rose, with far more deference than he deserved.

"Look, in the first place," he replied, "how intolerably straight against the sky is the line of the hill. It would need breaking up and diversifying. And where we are standing the whole thing is out of perspective. Besides, all the coloring is monotonous and crude."

"I do not know anything about pictures," I put in, "and I do not pretend to know: but I know what is beautiful when I see it, and I am thoroughly content with this."

"Indeed, who could help being contented!" said the elder Miss Robinson; and Mr. Sandbach said the same.

"Ah!" said Leyland, "you all confuse the artistic view of Nature with the photographic."

Poor Rose had brought her camera with her, so I thought this positively rude. I did not wish any unpleasantness: so I merely turned away and assisted my wife and Miss Mary Robinson to put out the lunch – not a very nice lunch.

"Eustace, dear," said his aunt, "come and help us here."

He was in a particularly bad temper that morning. He had, as usual, not wanted to come, and his aunts had nearly allowed him to stop at the hotel to vex Janet. But I, with their permission, spoke to him rather sharply on the subject of exercise; and the result was that he had come, but was even more taciturn and moody than usual.

Obedience was not his strong point. He invariably questioned every command, and only executed it grumbling. I should always insist on prompt and cheerful obedience, if I had a son.

"I'm – coming – Aunt – Mary," he at last replied, and dawdled to cut a piece of wood to make a whistle, taking care not to arrive till we had finished.

"Well, well, sir!" said I, "you stroll in at the end and profit by our labors." He sighed, for he could not endure being chaffed. Miss Mary, very unwisely, insisted on giving him the wing of the chicken, in spite of all my attempts to prevent her. I remember that I had a moment's vexation when I thought that, instead of enjoying the sun, and the air, and the woods, we were all engaged in wrangling over the diet of a spoilt boy.

But, after lunch, he was a little less in evidence. He withdrew to a tree trunk, and began to loosen the bark from his whistle. I was thankful to see him employed, for once in a way. We reclined, and took a dolce far niente.

Those sweet chestnuts of the South are puny striplings compared with our robust Northerners. But they clothed the contours of the hills and valleys in a most pleasing way, their veil being only broken by two clearings, in one which we were sitting.

And because these few trees were cut down, Leyland burst into a petty indictment of the proprietor.

"All the poetry is going from Nature," he cried, "her lakes and marshes are drained, her seas banked up, her forests cut down. Everywhere we see the vulgarity of desolation spreading."

I have had some experience of estates, and answered that cutting was very necessary for the health of the larger trees. Besides, it was unreasonable to expect the proprietor to derive no income from his lands.

"If you take the commercial side of landscape, you may feel pleasure in the owner's activity. But to me the mere thought that a tree is convertible into cash is disgusting."

"I see no reason," I observed politely, "to despise the gifts of Nature because they are of value."

It did not stop him. "It is no matter," he went on, "we are all hopelessly steeped in vulgarity. I do not except myself. It is through us, and to our shame, that the Nereids have left the waters and the Oreads the mountains, that the woods no longer give shelter to Pan."

"Pan!" cried Mr. Sandbach, his mellow voice filling the valley as if it had been a great green church, "Pan is dead. That is why the woods do not shelter him." And he began to tell the striking story of the mariners who were sailing near the coast at the time of the birth of Christ, and three times heard a loud voice saying: "The great God Pan is dead."

"Yes. The great God Pan is dead," said Leyland. And he abandoned himself to that mock misery in which artistic people are so fond of indulging. His cigar went out, and he had to ask me for a match.

"How very interesting," said Rose. "I do wish I knew some ancient history."

"It is not worth your notice," said Mr. Sandbach. "Eh, Eustace?"

Eustace was finishing his whistle. He looked up, with the irritable frown in which his aunts allowed him to indulge, and made no reply.

The conversation turned to various topics and then died out. It was a cloudless afternoon in May, and the pale green of the young chestnut leaves made a pretty contrast with the dark blue of the sky. We were all sitting at the edge of the small clearing for the sake of the view, and the shade of the chestnut saplings behind us was manifestly insufficient. All sounds died away – at least that is my account: Miss Robinson says that the clamor of the birds was the first sign of uneasiness that she discerned. All sounds died away, except that, far in the distance, I could hear two boughs of a great chestnut grinding together as the tree swayed. The grinds grew shorter and shorter, and finally that sound stopped also. As I looked over the green fingers of the valley, everything was absolutely motionless and still; and that feeling of suspense which one so often experiences when Nature is in repose, began to steal over me.

Suddenly, we were all electrified by the excruciating noise of Eustace's whistle. I never heard any instrument give forth so ear-splitting and discordant a sound.

"Eustace, dear," said Miss Mary Robinson, "you might have thought of your poor Aunt Julia's head."

Leyland, who had apparently been asleep, sat up.

"It is astonishing how blind a boy is to anything that is elevating or beautiful," he observed. "I should not have thought he could have found the wherewithal out here to spoil our pleasure like this."

Then the terrible silence fell upon us again. I was now standing up and watching a catspaw of wind that was running down one of the ridges opposite, turning the light green to dark as it traveled. A fanciful feeling of foreboding came over me; so I turned away, to find to my amazement, that all the others were also on their feet, watching it too.

It is not possible to describe coherently what happened next: but I, for one, am not ashamed to confess that, though the fair blue sky was above me, and the green spring woods beneath me, and the kindest of friends around me, yet I became terribly frightened, more frightened than I ever wish to become again, frightened in a way I never have known either before or after. And in the eyes of the others, too, I saw blank, expressionless fear, while their mouths strove in vain to speak and their hands to gesticulate. Yet, all around us were prosperity, beauty, and peace, and all was motionless, save the catspaw of wind, now traveling up the ridge on which we stood.

Who moved first has never been settled. It is enough to say that in one second we were tearing away along the hillside. Leyland was in front, then Mr. Sandbach, then my wife. But I only saw for a brief moment; for I ran across the little clearing and through the woods and over the undergrowth and the rocks and down the dry torrent beds into the valley below. The sky might have been black as I ran, and the trees short grass, and the hillside a level road; for I saw nothing and heard nothing and felt nothing, since all the channels of sense and reason were blocked. It was not the spiritual fear that one has known at other times, but brutal overmastering physical fear, stopping up the ears, and dropping clouds before the eyes, and filling the mouth with foul tastes. And it was no ordinary humiliation that survived; for I had been afraid, not a man, but as a beast.

II.

I cannot describe our finish any better than our start; for our fear passed away as it had come, without cause. Suddenly I was able to see, and hear, and cough, and clear my mouth. Looking back, I saw that the others were stopping too; and, in a short time, we were all together, though it was long before we could speak, and longer before we dared to.

No one was seriously injured. My poor wife had sprained her ankle, Leyland had torn one of his nails on a tree trunk, and I myself had scraped and damaged my ear. I never noticed it till I had stopped.

We were all silent, searching one another's faces. Suddenly Miss Mary Robinson gave a terrible shriek. "Oh, merciful heavens! where is Eustace?" And then she would have fallen, if Mr. Sandbach had not caught her.

"We must go back, we must go back at once," said my Rose, who was quite the most collected of the party. "But I hope – I feel he is safe."

Such was the cowardice of Leyland, that he objected. But, finding himself in a minority, and being afraid of being left alone, he gave in. Rose and I supported my poor wife, Mr. Sandbach and Miss Robinson helped Miss Mary, and we returned slowly and silently, taking forty minutes to ascend the path that we had descended in ten.

Our conversation was naturally disjointed, as no one wished to offer an opinion on what had happened. Rose was the most talkative: she startled us all by saying that she had very nearly stopped where she was.

"Do you mean to say that you weren't – that you didn't feel compelled to go?" said Mr. Sandbach.

"Oh, of course, I did feel frightened" – she was the first to use the word – "but I somehow felt that if I could stop on it would be quite different, that I shouldn't be frightened at all, so to speak." Rose never did express herself clearly: still, it is greatly to her credit that she, the youngest of us, should have held on so long at that terrible time.

"I should have stopped, I do believe," she continued, "if I had not seen mamma go."

Rose's experience comforted us a little about Eustace. But a feeling of terrible foreboding was on us all, as we painfully climbed the chestnut-covered slopes and neared the little clearing. When we reached it our tongues broke loose. There, at the further side, were the remains of our lunch, and close to them, lying motionless on his back, was Eustace.

With some presence of mind I at once cried out: "Hey, you young monkey! jump up!" But he made no reply, nor did he answer when his poor aunts spoke to him. And, to my unspeakable horror, I saw one of those green lizards dart out from under his shirt-cuff as we approached.

We stood watching him as he lay there so silently, and my ears began to tingle in expectation of the outbursts of lamentations and tears.

Miss Mary fell on her knees beside him and touched his hand, which was convulsively entwined in the long grass.

As she did so, he opened his eyes and smiled.

I have often seen that peculiar smile since, both on the possessor's face and on the photographs of him that are beginning to get into the illustrated papers. But, till then, Eustace had always worn a peevish, discontented frown; and we were all unused to this disquieting smile, which always seemed to be without adequate reason.

His aunts showered kisses on him, which he did not reciprocate, and then there was an awkward pause. Eustace seemed so natural and undisturbed; yet, it he had not had astonishing experiences himself, he ought to have been all the more astonished at our extraordinary behavior. My wife, with ready tact, endeavored to behave as it nothing had happened.

"Well, Mr. Eustace," she said, sitting down as she spoke, to ease her foot, "how have you been amusing yourself since we have been away?"

"Thank you, Mrs. Tytler, I have been very happy."

"And where have you been?"

"Here."

"And lying down all the time, you idle boy?"

"No, no! all the time."

"What were you doing before?"

"Oh; standing or sitting."

"Stood and sat doing nothing! Don't you know the poem 'Satan finds some mischief still for – '"

"Oh, my dear madam, hush! hush!" Mr. Sandbach's voice broke in; and my wife, naturally mortified by the interruption, said no more and moved away. I was surprised to see Rose immediately take her place, and, with more freedom than she generally displayed, run her fingers through the boy's tousled hair.

"Eustace! Eustace!" she said, hurriedly, "tell me everything – every single thing."

Slowly he sat up – till then he had lain on his back.

"Oh Rose," he whispered, and, my curiosity being aroused, I moved nearer to hear what he was going to say. As I did so, I caught sight of some goats' footmarks in the moist earth beneath the trees.

"Apparently you have had a visit from some goats," I observed. "I had no idea they fed up here."

Eustace laboriously got on to his feet and came to see; and when he saw the footmarks he lay down and rolled on them, as a dog rolls in dirt.

After that there was a grave silence, broken at length by the solemn speech of Mr. Sandbach.

"My dear friends," he said, "it is best to confess the truth bravely. I know that what I am going to say now is what you are all now feeling. The Evil One has been very near us in bodily form. Time may yet discover some injury that he has wrought among us. But, at present, for myself at all events, I wish to offer up thanks for a merciful deliverance."

With that he knelt down, and, as the others knelt, I knelt too, though I do not believe in the Devil being allowed to assail us in visible form, as I told Mr. Sandbach afterwards. Eustace came too, and knelt quietly enough between his aunts after they had beckoned to him. But when it was over he at once got up, and began hunting for something.

"Why! Someone has cut my whistle in two," he said. (I had seen Leyland with an open knife in his hand – a superstitious act which I could hardly approve.)

"Well, it doesn't matter," he continued.

"And why doesn't it matter?" said Mr. Sandbach, who has ever since tried to entrap Eustace into an account of that mysterious hour.

"Because I don't want it any more."

"Why?"

At that he smiled; and, as no one seemed to have anything more to say, I set off as fast as I could through the wood, and hauled up a donkey to carry my poor wife home. Nothing occurred in my absence, except that Rose had asked Eustace to tell her what had happened; and he, this time, had turned away his head, and had not answered her a single word.

As soon as I returned, we all set off. Eustace walked with difficulty, almost with pain, so that, when we reached the other donkeys, his aunts wished him to mount one of them and ride all the way home. I make it a rule never to interfere between relatives, but I put my foot down at this. As it turned out, I was perfectly right, for the healthy exercise, I suppose, began to thaw Eustace's sluggish blood and loosen his stiffened muscles. He stepped out manfully, for the first time in his life, holding his head up and taking deep drafts of air into his chest. I observed with satisfaction to Miss Mary Robinson, that Eustace was at last taking some pride in his personal appearance.

Mr. Sandbach sighed, and said that Eustace must be carefully watched, for we none of us understood him yet. Miss Mary Robinson being very much – over much, I think – guided by him, sighed too.

"Come, come, Miss Robinson," I said, "there's nothing wrong with Eustace. Our

experiences are mysterious, not his. He was astonished at our sudden departure, that's why he was so strange when we returned. He's right enough – improved, if anything."

"And is the worship of athletics, the cult of insensate activity, to be counted as an improvement?" put in Leyland, fixing a large, sorrowful eye on Eustace, who had stopped to scramble on to a rock to pick some cyclamen. "The passionate desire to rend from Nature the few beauties that have been still left her – that is to be counted as an improvement too?"

It is mere waste of time to reply to such remarks, especially when they come from an unsuccessful artist, suffering from a damaged finger. I changed the conversation by asking what we should say at the hotel. After some discussion, it was agreed that we should say nothing, either there or in our letters home. Importunate truthtelling, which brings only bewilderment and discomfort to the hearers, is, in my opinion, a mistake; and, after a long discussion, I managed make Mr. Sandbach acquiesce in my view.

Eustace did not share in our conversation. He was racing about, like a real boy, in the wood to the right. A strange feeling of shame prevented us from openly mentioning our fright to him. Indeed, it seemed almost reasonable to conclude that it had made but little impression on him. So it disconcerted us when he bounded back with an armful of flowering acanthus, calling out:

"Do you suppose Gennaro'll be there when we get back?"

Gennaro was the stop-gap waiter, a clumsy, impertinent fisher-lad, who had been had up from Minori in the absence of the nice English-speaking Emmanuele. It was to him that we owed our scrappy lunch; and I could not conceive why Eustace desired to see him, unless it was to make mock with him of our behavior.

"Yes, of course he will be there," said Miss Robinson. "Why do you ask, dear?"

"Oh, I thought I'd like to see him."

"And why?" snapped Mr. Sandbach.

"Because, because I do, I do; because, because I do." He danced away into the darkening wood to the rhythm of his words.

"This is very extraordinary," said Mr. Sandbach. "Did he like Gennaro before?"

"Gennaro has only been here two days," said Rose, "and I know that they haven't spoken to each other a dozen times."

Each time Eustace returned from the wood his spirits were higher. Once he came whooping down on us as a wild Indian, and another time he made believe to be a dog . The last time he came back with a poor dazed hare, too frightened to move, sitting on his arm. He was getting too uproarious, I thought; and we were all glad to leave the wood, and start upon the steep staircase path that leads down into Ravello. It was late and turning dark; and we made all the speed we could, Eustace scurrying in front of us like a goat.

Just where the staircase path debouches on the white high road, the next extraordinary incident of this extraordinary day occurred. Three old women were standing by the wayside. They, like ourselves, had come down from the woods, and they were resting their heavy bundles of fuel on the low parapet of the road. Eustace stopped in front of them, and, after a moment's deliberation, stepped forward and – kissed the left-hand one on the cheek!

"My good fellow!" exclaimed Mr. Sandbach, "are you quite crazy?"

Eustace said nothing, but offered the old woman some of his flowers, and then hurried on. I looked back; and the old woman's companions seemed as much astonished at the proceeding as we were. But she herself had put the flowers in her bosom, and was murmuring blessings.

This salutation of the old lady was the first example of Eustace's strange behavior, and we were both surprised and alarmed. It was useless talking to him, for he either made silly replies, or else bounded away without replying at all.

He made no reference on the way home to Gennaro, and I hoped that that was forgotten. But, when we came to the Piazza, in front of the Cathedral, he screamed out: "Gennaro! Gennaro!" at the top of his voice, and began running up the little alley that led to the hotel. Sure enough, there was Gennaro at the end of it, with his arms and legs sticking out of the nice little English-speaking waiter's dress suit, and a dirty fisherman's cap on his head – for, as the poor landlady truly said, however much she superintended his toilette, he always managed to introduce something incongruous into it before he had done.

Eustace sprang to meet him, and leapt right up into his arms, and put his own arms round his neck. And this in the presence, not only of us, but also of the landlady, the chambermaid, the facchino, and of two American ladies who were coming for a few days' visit to the little hotel.

I always make a point of behaving pleasantly to Italians, however little they may deserve it; but this habit of promiscuous intimacy was perfectly intolerable, and could only lead to familiarity and mortification for all. Taking Miss Robinson aside, I asked her permission to speak seriously to Eustace on the subject of intercourse with social inferiors. She granted it; but I determined to wait till the absurd boy had calmed down a little from the excitement of the day. Meanwhile, Gennaro, instead of attending to the wants of the two new ladies, carried Eustace into the house, as if it was the most natural thing in the world.

"Ho capito," I heard him say as he passed me. 'Ho capito' is the Italian for ' I have understood'; but, as Eustace had not spoken to him, I could not see the force of the remark. It served to increase our bewilderment, and, by the time we sat down at the dinner table, our imaginations and our tongues were alike exhausted.

I omit from this account the various comments that were made, as few of them seem worthy of being recorded. But, for three or four hours, seven of us were pouring forth our bewilderment in a stream of appropriate and inappropriate exclamations. Some traced a connection between our behavior in the afternoon and the behavior of Eustace now. Others saw no connection at all. Mr. Sandbach still held to the possibility of infernal influences, and also said that he ought to have a doctor. Leyland only saw the development of "that unspeakable Philistine, the boy." Rose maintained, to my surprise, that everything was excusable; while I began to see that the young gentleman wanted a sound thrashing. The poor Miss Robinsons swayed helplessly about between these diverse opinions; inclining now to careful supervision, now to acquiescence, now to corporal chastisement, now to Eno's Fruit Salt.

Dinner passed off fairly well, though Eustace was terribly fidgety, Gennaro as usual dropping the knives and spoons, and hawking and clearing his throat. He only knew a few words of English, and we were all reduced to Italian for making known our wants. Eustace, who had picked up a little somehow, asked for some oranges. To my annoyance, Gennaro, in his answer made use of the second person singular – a form only used when addressing those who are both intimates and equals. Eustace had brought it on himself; but an impertinence of this kind was an affront to all, and I was determined to speak, and to speak at once.

When I heard him clearing the table I went in, and, summoning up my Italian, or rather Neapolitan – the Southern dialect- are execrable – I said, "Gennaro! I heard you address Signor Eustace with 'Tu.'"

"It is true."

"You are not right. You must use 'Lei' or 'Voi' – more polite forms. And remember that, though Signor Eustace is sometimes silly and foolish – this afternoon for example – yet you must always behave respectfully to him; for he is a young English gentleman, and you are a poor Italian fisherboy."

I know that speech sounds terribly snobbish, but in Italian one can say things that one would never dream of saying in English. Besides, it is no speaking delicately to persons of that class. Unless you put things plainly, they take a vicious pleasure in misunderstanding you.

An honest English fisherman would have landed me one in the eye in a minute for such a remark, but the wretched down-trodden Italians have no pride. Gennaro only sighed, and said: "It is true."

"Quite so," I said, and turned to go. To my indignation I heard him add: "But sometimes it is not important."

"What do you mean?" I shouted.

He came close up to me with horrid gesticulating fingers.

"Signor Tytler, I wish to say this. If Eustazio asks me to call him 'Voi,' I will call
 him 'Voi.' Otherwise, no."

With that he seized up a tray of dinner things, and fled from the room with them; and I heard two more wine-glasses go on the courtyard floor.

I was now fairly angry, and strode out to interview Eustace. But he had gone to bed, and the landlady, to whom I also wished to speak, was engaged. After more vague wonderings, obscurely expressed owing to the presence of Janet and the two American ladies, we all went to bed, too, after a harassing and most extraordinary day.

III.

But the day was nothing to the night.

I suppose I had slept for about four hours, when I woke suddenly thinking I heard a noise in the garden. And immediately, before my eyes were open, cold terrible fear seized me – not fear of something that was happening, like the fear in the wood, but fear of something that might happen.

Our room was on the first floor, looking out on to the garden – or terrace, it was rather: a wedge-shaped block of ground covered with roses and vines, and intersected with little asphalt paths. It was bounded on the small side by the house; round the two long sides ran a wall, only three feet above the terrace level, but with a good twenty feet drop over it into the olive yards, for the ground fell very precipitously away.

Trembling all over I stole to the window. There, pattering up and down the asphalt paths, was something white. I was too much alarmed to see clearly; and in the uncertain light of the stars the thing took all manner of curious shape. Now it was a great dog, now an enormous white bat, now a mass of quickly traveling cloud. It would bounce like a ball, or take short flights like a bird, or glide slowly like a wraith. It gave no sound save the pattering sound of what, after all, must be human feet. And at last the obvious explanation forced itself upon my disordered mind; and I realized that Eustace had got out of bed, and that we were in for something more.

I hastily dressed myself, and went down into the dining-room which opened upon the terrace. The door was already unfastened. My terror had almost entirely passed away, but for quite five minutes I struggled with a curious cowardly feeling, which bade me not interfere with the poor strange boy, but leave him to his ghostly patterings, and merely watch him from the window, to see he took no harm.

But better impulses prevailed and, opening the door, I called out: "Eustace! what on earth are you doing? Come in at once."

He stopped his antics, and said: "I hate my bedroom. I could not stop in it, it is too small."

"Come! come! I'm tired of affectation. You've never complained of it before."

"Besides I can't see anything – no flowers, no leaves, no sky: only a stone wall." The outlook of Eustace's room certainly was limited; but, as I told him, he had never complained of it before.

"Eustace, you talk like a child. Come in! Prompt obedience, if you please."

He did not move.

"Very well: I shall carry you in by force," I added, and made a few steps towards him. But I was soon convinced of the futility of pursuing a boy through a tangle of asphalt paths and went in instead, to call Mr. Sandbach and Leyland to my aid.

When I returned with them he was worse than ever. He would not even answer us when we spoke, but began singing and chattering to himself in a most alarming way.

"It's a case for the doctor now," said Mr. Sandbach, gravely tapping his forehead.

He had stopped his running and was singing, first low, then loud – singing five-finger exercises, scales, hymn tunes, scraps of Wagner – anything that came into his head. His voice – a very untuneful voice – grew stronger and stronger, and he ended with a tremendous shout which boomed like a gun among the mountains, and awoke everyone who was still sleeping in the hotel. My poor wife and the two girls appeared at their respective windows, and the American ladies were heard violently ringing their bell.

"Eustace," we all cried, "stop! stop, dear boy, and come into the house."

He shook his head, and started off again – talking this time. Never have I listened to such an extraordinary speech. At any other time it would have been ludicrous, for here was a boy, with no sense of beauty and a puerile command of words, attempting to tackle themes which the greatest poets have found almost beyond their power. Eustace Robinson, aged fourteen, was standing in his nightshirt saluting, praising, and blessing, the great forces and manifestations of Nature.

He spoke first of night and the stars and planets above his head, of the swarms of fireflies below him, of the invisible sea below the fireflies, of the great rocks covered with anemones and shells that were slumbering in the invisible sea. He spoke of the rivers and waterfalls, of the ripening bunches of grapes, of the smoking cone of Vesuvius and the hidden fire-channels that made the smoke, of the myriads of lizards who were lying curled up in the crannies of the sultry earth, of the showers of white rose-leaves that were tangled in his hair. And then he spoke of the rain and the wind by which all things are changed, of the air through which all things live, and of the woods in which all things can be hidden.

Of course, it was all absurdly high-faluting: yet I could have kicked Leyland for audibly observing that it was 'a diabolical caricature of all that was most holy and beautiful in life.'

"And then," – Eustace was going on in the pitiable conversational doggerel which was his only mode of expression – "and then there are men, but I can't make them out so well." He knelt down by the parapet, and rested his head on his arms.

"Now's the time," whispered Leyland. I hate stealth, hut we darted forward and endeavored to catch hold of him from behind. He was away in a twinkling, but turned round at once to look at us. As far as I could see in the starlight, he was crying. Leyland rushed at him again, and we tried to corner him among the asphalt paths, hut without the slightest approach to success.

We returned, breathless and discomfited, leaving him to his madness in the further
corner of the terrace. But my Rose had an inspiration.

"Papa," she called from the window, "if you get Gennaro, he might he able to catch him for you."

I had no wish to ask a favor of Gennaro, but, as the landlady had by now appeared on the scene, I begged her to summon him from the charcoal-bin in which he slept, and make him try what he could do.

She soon returned, and was shortly followed by Gennaro, attired in a dress coat, without either waistcoat, shirt, or vest, and a ragged pair of what had been trousers, cut short above the knees for purposes of wading. The landlady, who had quite picked up English ways, rebuked him for the incongruous and even indecent appearance which he presented.

"I have a coat and I have trousers. What more do you desire?"

"Never mind, Signora Scafetti," I put in. "As there are no ladies here, it is not of the slightest consequence." Then, turning to Gennaro, I said: "The aunts of Signor Eustace wish you to fetch him into the house."

He did not answer.

"Do you hear me? He is not well. I order you to fetch him into the house."

"Fetch! fetch!" said Signora Scafetti, and shook him roughly by the arm.

"Eustazio is well where he is."

"Fetch! fetch!" Signora Scafetti screamed, and let loose a flood of Italian, most of which, I am glad to say, I could not follow. I glanced up nervously at the girls' window, but they hardly know as much as I do, and I am thankful to say that none of us caught one word of Gennaro's answer.

The two yelled and shouted at each other for quite ten minutes, at the end of which Gennaro rushed hack to his charcoal-bin and Signora Scafetti burst into tears, as well she might, for she greatly valued her English guests .

"He says," she sobbed, "that Signor Eustace is well where he is, and that he will not fetch him. I can do no more."

But I could, for, in my stupid British way, I have got some insight into the Italian character. I followed Mr. Gennaro to his place of repose, and found him wriggling down on a dirty sack.

"I wish you to fetch Signor Eustace to me," I began.

He hurled at me an unintelligible reply.

"If you fetch him, I will give you this." And out of my pocket I took a new ten lira note.

This time he did not answer.

"This note is equal to ten lire in silver," I continued, for I knew that the poor-class Italian is unable to conceive of a single large sum.

"I know it."

"That is, two hundred soldi."

"I do not desire them. Eustazio is my friend."

I put the note into my pocket.

"Besides, you would not give it me."

"I am an Englishman. The English always do what they promise."

"That is true." It is astonishing how the most dishonest of nations trust us. Indeed they often trust us more than we trust one another. Gennaro knelt up on his sack. It was too dark to see his face, but I could feel his warm garlicky breath coming out in gasps, and I knew that the eternal avarice of the South had laid hold upon him.

"I could not fetch Eustazio to the house. He might die there."

"You need not do that," I replied patiently. "You need only bring him to me; and I will stand outside in the garden." And to this, as if it were something quite different, the pitiable youth consented.

"But give me first the ten lire."

"No " – for I knew the kind of person with which I had to deal. Once faithless, always faithless.

We returned to the terrace, and Gennaro, without a single word, pattered off towards the pattering that could be heard at the remoter end. Mr. Sandbach, Leyland, and myself moved away a little from the house, and stood in the shadow of the white climbing roses, practically invisible.

We heard "Eustazio" called, followed by absurd cries of pleasure from the poor boy. The pattering ceased, and we heard them talking. Their voices got nearer, and presently I could discern them through the creep the grotesque figure of the young man, and the slim little white-robed boy. Gennaro had his arm round Eustace's neck, and Eustace was talking away in his fluent, slipshod Italian.

"I understand almost everything," I heard him say. "The trees, hills, stars, water, I can see all. But isn't it odd! I can't make out men a bit. Do you know what I mean?"

"Ho capito," said Gennaro gravely, and took his arm off Eustace's shoulder. But I

made the new note crackle in my pocket; and he heard it. He stuck his hand out with a jerk; and the unsuspecting Eustace gripped it in his own.

"It is odd!" Eustace went on – they were quite close now – "It almost seems as if – as if –"

I darted out and caught hold of his arm, and Leyland got hold of the other arm, and Mr. Sandbach hung on to his feet. He gave shrill heart-piercing screams; and the white roses, which were falling early that year, descended in showers on him as we dragged him into the house.

As soon as we entered the house he stopped shrieking; but floods of tears silently burst forth, and spread over his upturned face.

"Not to my room," he pleaded. "It is so small."

His infinitely dolorous look filled me with strange pity, but what could I do? Besides, his window was the only one that had bars to it.

"Never mind, dear boy," said kind Mr. Sandbach. "I will bear you company till the morning."

At this his convulsive struggles began again. "Oh, please, not that. Anything but that. I will promise to lie still and not to cry more than I can help, if I am left alone."

So we laid him on the bed, and drew the sheets over him, and left him sobbing bitterly, and saying: "I nearly saw everything, and now I can see nothing at all."

We informed the Miss Robinsons of all that had happened, and returned to the dining-room, where we found Signora Scafetti and Gennaro whispering together. Mr. Sandbach got pen and paper, and began writing to the English doctor at Naples. I at once drew out the note, and flung it down on the table to Gennaro.

"Here is your pay," I said sternly, for I was thinking of the Thirty Pieces of Silver.

"Thank you very much, sir," said Gennaro, and grabbed it.

He was going off, when Leyland, whose interest and indifference were always equally misplaced, asked him what Eustace had meant by saying 'he could not make out men a bit.'

"I cannot say. Signor Eustazio" (I was glad to observe a little deference at last) "has a subtle brain. He understands many things."

"But I heard you say you understood," Leyland persisted.

"I understand, but I cannot explain. I am a poor Italian fisher-lad. Yet, listen: I will try." I saw to my alarm that his manner was changing, and tried to stop him. But he sat down on the edge of the table and started off, with some absolutely incoherent remarks.

"It is sad," he observed at last. "What has happened is very sad. But what can I do? I am poor. It is not I."

I turned away in contempt. Leyland went on asking questions. He wanted to know who it was that Eustace had in his mind when he spoke.

"That is easy to say," Gennaro gravely answered. "It is you, it is I. It is all in this house, and many outside it. If he wishes for mirth, we discomfort him. If he asks to be alone, we disturb him. He longed for a friend, and found none for fifteen years. Then he found me, and the first night I – I who have been in the woods and understood things too – betray him to you, and send him in to die. But what could I do?"

"Gently, gently," said I.

"Oh, assuredly he will die. He will lie in the small room all night, and in the morning he will be dead. That I know for certain."

"There, that will do," said Mr. Sandbach. "I shall be sitting with him."

"Filomena Giusti sat all night with Caterina, but Caterina was dead in the morning. They would not let her out, though I begged, and prayed, and cursed, and beat the door, and climbed the wall. They were ignorant fools, and thought I wished to carry her away. And in the morning she was dead."

"What is all this?" I asked Signora Scafetti.

"All kinds of stories will get about," she replied, "and he, least of anyone, has reason to repeat them."

"And I am alive now," he went on, "because I had neither parents nor relatives nor friends, so that, when the first night came, I could run through the woods, and climb the rocks, and plunge into the water, until I had accomplished my desire!"

We heard a cry from Eustace's room – a faint but steady sound, like the sound of wind in a distant wood heard by one standing in tranquility.

"That," said Gennaro, "was the last noise of Caterina. I was hanging on to her window then, and it blew out past me."

And, lilting up his hand, in which my ten lira note was safely packed, he solemnly cursed Mr. Sandbach, and Leyland, and myself, and Fate, because Eustace was dying in the upstairs room. Such is the working of the Southern mind; and I verily believe that he would not have moved even then, had not Leyland, that unspeakable idiot, upset the lamp with his elbow. It was a patent self-extinguishing lamp, bought by Signora Scafetti, at my special request, to replace the dangerous thing that she was using. The result was, that it went out; and the mere physical change from light to darkness had more power over the ignorant animal nature of Gennaro than the most obvious dictates of logic and reason. I felt, rather than saw, that he had left the room and shouted out to Mr. Sandbach: "Have you got the key of Eustace's room in your pocket?" But Mr. Sandbach and Leyland were both on the floor, having mistaken each other for Gennaro, and some more precious time was wasted in finding a match. Mr. Sandbach had only just time to say that he had left the key in the door, in case the Miss Robinsons wished to pay Eustace a visit, when we heard a noise on the stairs, and there was Gennaro, carrying Eustace down.

We rushed out and blocked up the passage, and they lost heart and retreated to the upper landing.

"Now they are caught," cried Signora Scafetti. "There is no other way out."

We were cautiously ascending the staircase, when there was a terrific scream from my wife's room, followed by a heavy thud on the asphalt path. They had leapt out of her window.

I reached the terrace just in time to see Eustace jumping over the parapet of the garden wall. This time I knew for certain he would be killed. But he alighted in an olive tree, looking like a great white moth, and from the tree he slid on to the earth. And as soon as his bare feet touched the clods of earth he uttered a strange loud cry, such as I should not have thought the human voice could have produced, and disappeared among the trees below.

"He has understood and he is saved," cried Gennaro, who was still sitting on the asphalt path. "Now, instead of dying he will live!"

"And you, instead of keeping the ten lire, will give them up." I retorted, for at this

theatrical remark I could contain myself no longer.

"The ten lire are mine," he hissed back, in a scarcely audible voice. He clasped his hand over his breast to protect his ill-gotten gains, and, as he did so, he swayed forward and fell upon his face on the path. He had not broken any limbs, and a leap like that would never have killed an Englishman, for the drop was not great. But those miserable Italians have no stamina. Something had gone wrong inside him, and he was dead.

The morning was still far off, but the morning breeze had begun, and more rose leaves fell on us as we carried him in. Signora Scafetti burst into screams at the sight of the dead body, and, far down the valley towards the sea, there still resounded the shouts and the laughter of the escaping boy.

The Other Side of the Hedge

My pedometer told me that I was twenty-five; and, though it is a shocking thing to stop walking, I was so tired that I sat down on a milestone to rest. People outstripped me, jeering as they did so, but I was too apathetic to feel resentful, and even when Miss Eliza Dimbleby, the great educationist, swept past, exhorting me to persevere, I only smiled and raised my hat.

At first I thought I was going to be like my brother, whom I had had to leave by the roadside a year or two round the corner. He had wasted his breath on singing, and his strength on helping others. But I had traveled more wisely, and now it was only the monotony of the highway that oppressed me – dust under foot and brown crackling hedges on either side, ever since I could remember.

And I had already dropped several things – indeed, the road behind was strewn with the things we all had dropped; and the white dust was settling down on them, so that already they looked no better than stones. My muscles were so weary that I could not even bear the weight of those things I still carried. I slid off the milestone into the road, and lay there prostrate, with my face to the great parched hedge, praying that I might give up.

A little puff of air revived me. It seemed to come from the hedge; and, when I opened my eyes, there was a glint of light through the tangle of boughs and dead leaves. The hedge could not be as thick as usual. In my weak, morbid state, I longed to force my way in, and see what was on the other side. No one was in sight, or I should not have dared to try. For we of the road do not admit in conversation that there is another side at all.

I yielded to the temptation, saying to myself that I would come back in a minute. The thorns scratched my face, and I had to use my arms as a shield, depending on my feet alone to push me forward. Halfway through I would have gone back, for in the passage all the things I was carrying were scraped off me, and my clothes were torn. But I was so wedged that return was impossible, and I had to wriggle blindly forward, expecting every moment that my strength would fail me, and that I should perish in the undergrowth.

Suddenly cold water closed round my head, and I seemed sinking down forever. I had fallen out of the hedge into a deep pool. I rose to the surface at last, crying for help, and I heard someone on the opposite bank laugh and say: "Another!" And then I was twitched out and laid panting on the dry ground.

Even when the water was out of my eyes, I was still dazed, for I had never been in so large a space, nor seen such grass and sunshine. The blue sky was no longer a strip, and beneath it the earth had risen grandly into hills – clean, bare buttresses, with beech trees in their folds, and meadows and clear pools at their feet. But the hills were not high, and there was in the landscape a sense of human occupation – so that one might have called it a park, or garden, if the words did not imply a certain triviality and constraint.

As soon as I got my breath, I turned to my rescuer and said: "Where does this place lead to?"

"Nowhere, thank the Lord!" said he, and laughed. He was a man of fifty or sixty – just the kind of age we mistrust on the road – but there was no anxiety in his manner, and his voice was that of a boy of eighteen.

"But it must lead somewhere!" I cried, too much surprised at his answer to thank him for saving my life.

"He wants to know where it leads!" he shouted to some men on the hillside, and they laughed back, and waved their caps.

I noticed then that the pool into which I had fallen was really a moat which bent round to the left and to the right, and that the hedge followed it continually. The hedge was green on this side – its roots showed through the clear water, and fish swam about in them – and it was wreathed over with dog-roses and traveler's joy. But it was a barrier, and in a moment I lost all pleasure in the grass, the sky, the trees, the happy men and women, and realized that the place was but a prison, for all its beauty and extent.

We moved away from the boundary, and then followed a path almost parallel to it, across the meadows. I found it difficult walking, for I was always trying to out-distance my companion, and there was no advantage in doing this if the place led nowhere. I had never kept step with anyone since I left my brother.

I amused him by stopping suddenly and saying disconsolately, "This is perfectly terrible. One cannot advance: one cannot progress. Now we of the road –"

"Yes. I know."

"I was going to say, we advance continually."

"I know."

"We are always learning, expanding, developing. Why, even in my short life I have seen a great deal of advance – the Transvaal War, the Fiscal Question, Christian Science, Radium. Here for example –"

I took out my pedometer, but it still marked twenty-five, not a degree more.

"Oh, it's stopped! I meant to show you. It should have registered all the time I was walking with you. But it makes me only twenty-five."

"Many things don't work in here," he said. "One day a man brought in a Lee-Metford, and that wouldn't work."

"The laws of science are universal in their application. It must be the water in the moat that has injured the machinery. In normal conditions everything works. Science and the spirit of emulation – those are the forces that have made us what we are."

I had to break off and acknowledge the pleasant greetings of people whom we passed. Some of them were singing, some talking, some engaged in gardening, hay-making, or other rudimentary industries. They all seemed happy; and I might have been happy too, if I could have forgotten that the place led nowhere.

I was startled by a young man who came sprinting across our path, took a little fence in fine style, and went tearing over a plowed field till he plunged into a lake, across which he began to swim. Here was true energy, and I exclaimed: "A cross-country race! Where are the others?"

"There are no others," my companion replied; and, later on, when we passed some long grass from which came the voice of a girl singing exquisitely to herself, he said again: "There are no others." I was bewildered at the waste in production, and murmured to myself, "What does it all mean?"

He said: "It means nothing but itself" – and he repeated the words slowly, as if I were a child.

"I understand," I said quietly, "but I do not agree. Every achievement is worthless unless it is a link in the chain of development. And I must not trespass on your kindness any longer. I must get back somehow to the road, and have my pedometer mended."

"First, you must see the gates," he replied, "for we have gates, though we never use them."

I yielded politely, and before long we reached the moat again, at a point where it was spanned by a bridge. Over the bridge was a big gate, as white as ivory, which was fitted into a gap in the boundary hedge. The gate opened outwards, and I exclaimed in amazement, for from it ran a road – just such a road as I had left – dusty under foot, with brown crackling hedges on either side as far as the eye could reach.

"That's my road!" I cried.

He shut the gate and said: "But not your part of the road. It is through this gate that humanity went out countless ages ago, when it was first seized with the desire to walk."

I denied this, observing that the part of the road I myself had left was not more than two miles off. But with the obstinacy of his years he repeated: "It is the same road. This is the beginning, and though it seems to run straight away from us, it doubles so often, that it is never far from our boundary and sometimes touches it." He stooped down by the moat, and traced on its moist margin an absurd figure like a maze. As we walked back through the meadows, I tried to convince him of his mistake.

"The road sometimes doubles, to be sure, but that is part of our discipline. Who can doubt that its general tendency is onward? To what goal we know not – it may be to some mountain where we shall touch the sky, it may be over precipices into the sea. But that it goes forward – who can doubt that? It is the thought of that that makes us strive to excel, each in his own way, and gives us an impetus which is lacking with you. Now that man who passed us – it's true that he ran well, and jumped well, and swam well; but we have men who can run better, and men who can jump better, and who can swim better. Specialization has produced results which would surprise you. Similarly, that girl –"

Here I interrupted myself to exclaim: "Good gracious me! I could have sworn it was Miss Eliza Dimbleby over there, with her feet in the fountain!"

He believed that it was.

"Impossible! I left her on the road, and she is due to lecture this evening at Tunbridge Wells. Why, her train leaves Cannon Street in – of course my watch has stopped like everything else. She is the last person to be here."

"People always are astonished at meeting each other. All kinds come through the hedge, and come at all times – when they are drawing ahead in the race, when they are lagging behind, when they are left for dead. I often stand near the boundary listening to the sounds of the road – you know what they are – and wonder if anyone will turn aside. It is my great happiness to help someone out of the moat, as I helped you. For our country fills up slowly, though it was meant for all mankind."

"Mankind have other aims," I said gently, for I thought him well-meaning; "and I must join them." I bade him good evening, for the sun was declining, and I wished to be on the road by nightfall. To my alarm, he caught hold of me, crying: "You are not to go yet!" I tried to shake him off, for we had no interests in common, and his civility was becoming irksome to me. But for all my struggles the tiresome old man would not let go; and, as wrestling is not my specialty, I was obliged to follow him.

It was true that I could have never found alone the place where I came in, and I hoped that, when I had seen the other sights about which he was worrying, he would take me back to it. But I was determined not to sleep in the country, for I mistrusted it, and the people too, for all their friendliness. Hungry though I was, I would not join them in their evening meals of milk and fruit, and, when they gave me flowers, I flung them away as soon as I could do so unobserved. Already they were lying down for the night like cattle – some out on the bare hillside, others in groups under the beeches. In the light of an orange sunset I hurried on with my unwelcome guide, dead tired, faint for want of food, but murmuring indomitably: "Give me life, with its struggles and victories, with its failures and hatreds, with its deep moral meaning and its unknown goal!"

At last we came to a place where the encircling moat was spanned by another bridge, and where another gate interrupted the line of the boundary hedge. It was different from the first gate; for it was half transparent like horn, and opened inwards. But through it, in the waning light, I saw again just such a road as I had left – monotonous, dusty, with brown crackling hedges on either side, as far as the eye could reach.

I was strangely disquieted at the sight, which seemed to deprive me of all self-control. A man was passing us, returning for the night to the hills, with a scythe over his shoulder and a can of some liquid in his hand. I forgot the destiny of our race. I forgot the road that lay before my eyes, and I sprang at him, wrenched the can out of his hand, and began to drink.

It was nothing stronger than beer, but in my exhausted state it overcame me in a moment. As in a dream, I saw the old man shut the gate, and heard him say: "This is where your road ends, and through this gate humanity – all that is left of it – will come in to us."

Though my senses were sinking into oblivion, they seemed to expand ere they reached it. They perceived the magic song of nightingales, and the odor of invisible hay, and stars piercing the fading sky. The man whose beer I had stolen lowered me down gently to sleep off its effects, and, as he did so, I saw that he was my brother.

The Celestial Omnibus

The boy who resided at Agathox Lodge, 28, Buckingham Park Road, Surbiton, had often been puzzled by the old signpost that stood almost opposite. He asked his mother about it, and she replied that it was a joke, and not a very nice one, which had been made many years back by some naughty young men, and that the police ought to remove it. For there were two strange things about this signpost: firstly, it pointed up a blank alley, and, secondly, it had painted on it, in faded characters, the words, "To Heaven."

"What kind of young men were they?" he asked.

"I think your father told me that one of them wrote verses, and was expelled from the University, and came to grief in other ways. Still, it was a long time ago. You must ask your father about it. He will say the same as I do, that it was put up as a joke."

"So it doesn't mean anything at all?"

She sent him upstairs to put on his best things, for the Bonses were coming to tea, and he was to hand the cake-stand.

It struck him, as he wrenched on his tightening trousers, that he might do worse than ask Mr. Bons about the signpost. His father, though very kind, always laughed at him – shrieked with laughter whenever he or any other child asked a question or spoke. But Mr. Bons was serious as well as kind. He had a beautiful house and lent one books, he was a churchwarden, and a candidate for the County Council; he had donated to the Free Library enormously, he presided over the Literary Society, and had Members of Parliament to stop with him – in short, he was probably the wisest person alive.

Yet even Mr. Bons could only say that the signpost was a joke – the joke of a person named Shelley.

"Of course!" cried the mother: "I told you so, dear. That was the name."

"Had you never heard of Shelley?" asked Mr. Bons.

"No," said the boy, and hung his head,

"But is there no Shelley in the house?"

"Why, yes!" exclaimed the lady, in much agitation. "Dear Mr. Bons, we aren't such Philistines as that. Two at the least. One a wedding present, and the other, smaller print, in one of the spare rooms."

"I believe we have seven Shelleys," said Mr. Bons, with a slow smile. Then he brushed the cake crumbs off his stomach – and, together with his daughter, rose to go.

The boy, obeying a wink from his mother, saw them all the way to the warden gate, and when they had gone he did not at once return to the house, but gazed for a little up and down Buckingham Park Road.

His parents lived at the right end of it. After No. 39 the quality of the houses dropped very suddenly, and 64 had not even a separate servants' entrance. But at the present moment the whole road looked rather pretty, for the sun had just set in splendor, and the inequalities of rent were drowned in a saffron afterglow. Small birds twittered, and the breadwinners' train shrieked musically down through the cutting – that wonderful cutting which has drawn to itself the whole beauty out of Surbiton. and clad itself, like any Alpine valley, with the glory of the fir and the silver birch and the primrose. It was this cutting that had first stirred desires within the boy – desires for something just a little different, he knew not what, desires that would return whenever things were sunlit as they were this evening, running up and down inside him, up and down, up and down. till he would feel quite unusual all over, and as likely as not would want to cry. This evening he was even sillier, for he slipped across the road towards the signpost and began to run up the blank alley.

The alley runs between high walls – the walls of the gardens of "Ivanhoe" and "Bella Vista" respectively. It smells a little all the way, and is scarcely twenty yards long. including the turn at the end. So not unnaturally the boy soon came to a standstill. "I'd like to kick that Shelley," he exclaimed, and glanced idly at a piece of paper which was pasted on the wall. Rather an odd piece of paper, and he read it carefully before he turned back. This is what he read:

S. and C.R.C.C.

Alteration in Service

Owing to lack of patronage the Company are regretfully compelled to suspend the hourly service, and to retain only the

Sunrise and Sunset Omnibuses,

which will run as usual. It is to be hoped that the public will patronize an arrangement which is intended for their convenience. As an extra inducement the Company will, for the first time, now issue

Return Tickets!

(available one day only), which may be obtained of the driver. Passengers are again reminded that no tickets are issued at the other end, and that no complaints in this connection will receive consideration from the Company. Nor will the Company be responsible for any negligence or stupidity on the part of Passengers, nor for Hailstorms, Lightning, Loss of Tickets, nor for any act of God.

For the Direction.

Now he had never seen this notice before, nor could he imagine where the omnibus went to. S, of course was for Surbiton, and R.C.C. meant Road Car Company. But what was the meaning of the other C.? Coombe and Maiden, perhaps, or possibly "City." Yet it could not hope to compete with the South-Western. The whole thing, the boy reflected, was run on hopelessly unbusiness-like lines. Why not tickets from the other end? And what an hour to start! Then he realized that unless the notice was a hoax. an omnibus must have been starting just as he was wishing the Bonses good-bye. He peered at the ground through the gathering dusk, and there he saw what might or might not be the marks of wheels. Yet nothing had come out of the alley. And he had never seen an omnibus at any time in the Buckingham Park Road. No, it must be a hoax, like the signposts – like the fairy tales, like the dreams upon which he would wake suddenly in the night. And with a sigh he stepped from the alley – right into the arms of his father.

Oh, how his father laughed! "Poor, poor Popsey!" he cried. "Diddums! Diddums! Diddums think he'd walky-palky up to Ewink!" And his mother, also convulsed with laughter, appeared on the steps of Agathox Lodge. "Don't, Bob!" she gasped. "Don't be so naughty! Oh, you'll kill me! Oh, leave the boy alone!"

But all that evening the joke was kept up. The father implored to be taken too. Was it a very tiring walk? Need one wipe one's shoes on the doormat? And the boy went to bed feeling faint and sore, and thankful for only one thing – that he had not said a word about the omnibus. It was a hoax, yet through his dreams it grew more and more real, and the streets of Surbiton, through which he saw it driving, seemed instead to become hoaxes and shadows. And very early in the morning he woke with a cry, for he had had a glimpse of its destination.

He struck a match, and its light fell not only on his watch but also on his calendar, so that he knew it to be half an hour to sunrise. It was pitch dark, for the fog had come down from London in the night, and all Surbiton was wrapped in its embrace. Yet he sprang out and dressed himself, for he was determined to settle once for all which was real: the omnibus or the streets. "I shall be a fool one way or the other," he thought. "Until I know." Soon he was shivering in the road under the gas lamp that guarded the entrance to the alley.

To enter the alley itself required some courage. Not only was it horribly dark, but he now realized that it was an impossible terminus for an omnibus. If it had not been for a policeman, whom he heard approaching through the fog, he would never have made the attempt. The next moment he had made the attempt and failed. Nothing. Nothing but a blank alley and a very silly boy gaping at its dirty floor. It was a hoax. "I'll tell papa and mamma," he decided. "I deserve it. I deserve that they should know. I am too silly to be alive." And he went back to the gate of Agathox Lodge. There he remembered that his watch was fast. The sun was not risen: it would not rise for two minutes. "Give the bus every chance," he thought cynically, and returned into the alley.

But the omnibus was there.

It had two horses, whose sides were still smoking from their journey, and its two great lamps shone through the fog against the alley's walls, changing their cobwebs and moss into tissues of fairyland. The driver was huddled up in a cape. He faced the blank wall, and how he had managed to drive in so neatly and so silently was one of the many things that the boy never discovered. Nor could he imagine how ever he would drive out.

"Please," his voice quavered through the foul brown air. "Please, is that an omnibus?" "Omnibus est," said the driver, without turning round. There was a moments silence. The policeman passed, coughing, by the entrance of the alley. The boy crouched in the shadow, for he did not want to be found out. He was pretty sure, too, that it was a Pirate; nothing else, he reasoned, would go from such odd places and at such odd hours.

"About when do you start?" He tried to sound nonchalant.

"At sunrise."

"How far do you go?"

"The whole way."

"And can I have a return ticket which will bring me all the way back?"

"You can."

"Do you know. I half think I'll come." The driver made no answer. The sun must have risen, for he unhitched the brake. And scarcely had the boy jumped in before the omnibus was off.

How? Did it turn? There was no room. Did it go forward? There was a blank wall. Yet it was moving – moving at a stately pace through the fog, which had turned from brown to yellow. The thought of warm bed and warmer breakfast made the boy feel faint. He wished he had not come.

His parents would not have approved. He would have gone back to them if the weather had not made it impossible, The solitude was terrible; he was the only passenger. And the omnibus, though well-built, was cold and somewhat musty. He drew his coat round him, and in so doing chanced to feel his pocket. It was empty. He had forgotten his purse.

"Stop!" he shouted. "Stop!" And then, being of a polite disposition, he glanced up at the painted notice-board so that he might call the driver by name. "Mr. Browne! stop; oh, do please stop!"

Mr. Browne did not stop, but he opened a little window and looked in at the boy. His face was a surprise – so kind it was and modest.

"Mr. Browne – I've left my purse behind. I've not got a penny. I can't pay for the ticket. Will you take my watch – please? I am in the most awful hole."

"Tickets on this line," said the driver, "whether single or return, can be purchased by coinage from no terrene mint. And a chronometer, though it had solaced the vigils of Charlemagne, or measured the slumbers of Laura, can acquire by no mutation the double-cake that charms the fangless Cerberus of Heaven!" So saying, he handed in the necessary ticket, and, while the boy said "Thank you," continued: "Titular pretensions. I know it well, are vanity. Yet they merit no censure when uttered on a laughing lip, and in an homonymous world are in some sort useful, since they do serve to distinguish one Jack from his fellow. Remember me. Therefore – as Sir Thomas Browne."

"Are you a Sir? Oh, sorry!" He had heard of these gentlemen drivers. "It is good of you about the ticket. But if you go on at this rate, however does your bus pay?"

"It does not pay. It was not intended to pay. Many are the faults of my equipage; it is compounded too curiously of foreign woods; its cushions tickle erudition rather than promote repose; and my horses are nourished not on the evergreen pastures of the moment, but on the dried bents and clovers of Latinity. But that it pays! – that error at all events was never intended and never attained."

"Sorry again –" said the boy rather hopelessly. Sir Thomas looked sad, fearing that, even for a moment, he had been the cause of sadness. He invited the boy to come up and sit beside him on the box, and together they journeyed on through the fog, which was now changing from yellow to white. There were no houses by the road; so it must be either Putney Heath or Wimbledon Common.

"Have you been a driver always?"

"I was a physician once."

"But why did you stop? Weren't you good?"

"As a healer of bodies I had scant success, and several score of my patients preceded me. But as a healer of the spirit I have succeeded beyond my hopes and my deserts. For though my drafts were not better nor subtler than those of other men, yet, by reason of the cunning goblets wherein I offered them, the queasy soul was ofttimes tempted to sip and be refreshed."

"The queasy soul" he murmured; "if the sun sets with trees in front of it, and you suddenly come strange all over, is that a queasy soul?"

"Have you felt that?"

"Why yes."

After a pause he told the boy a little, a very little, about the journey's end. But they did not chatter much, for the boy, when he liked a person, would as soon sit silent in his company as speak, and this, he discovered, was also the mind of Sir Thomas Browne and of many others with whom he was to be acquainted. He heard, however, about the young man Shelley, who was now quite a famous person, with a carriage of his own, and about some of the other drivers who are in the service of the Company. Meanwhile the light grew stronger, though the fog did not disperse. It was now more like mist than fog, and at times would travel quickly across them, as if it was part of a cloud. They had been ascending, too, in a most puzzling way; for over two hours the horses had been pulling against the collar, and even if it were Richmond Hill they ought to have been at the top long ago. Perhaps it was Epsom, or even the North Downs; yet the air seemed keener than that which blows on either. And as to the name of their destination. Sir Thomas Browne was silent.

Crash!

"Thunder, by Jove!" said the boy, "and not so far off either. Listen to the echoes! It's more like mountains."

He thought, not very vividly, of his father and mother. He saw them sitting down to sausages and listening to the storm. He saw his own empty place. Then there would be questions, alarms, theories, jokes, consolations. They would expect him back at lunch. To lunch he would not come, nor to tea, but he would be in for dinner, and so his day's truancy would be over. If he had had his purse he would have bought them presents – not that he should have known what to get them.

Crash!

The peal and the lightning came together. The cloud quivered as if it were alive; and torn streamers of mist rushed past. "Are you afraid?" asked Sir Thomas Browne.

"What is there to be afraid of? Is it much farther?"

The horses of the omnibus stopped just as a ball of fire burst up and exploded with a ringing noise that was deafening but clear, like the noise of a blacksmith's forge. All the cloud was shattered.

"Oh, listen, Sir Thomas Browne! No, I mean look; we shall get a view at last. No, I mean listen; that sounds like a rainbow!"

The noise had died into the faintest murmur, beneath which another murmur grew, spreading stealthily, steadily – in a curve that widened but did not vary. And in widening curves a rainbow was spreading from the horses' feet into the dissolving mists.

"But how beautiful! What colors! Where will it stop? It is more like the rainbows you can tread on. More like dreams."

The color and the sound grew together. The rainbow spanned an enormous gulf. Clouds rushed under it and were pierced by it, and still it grew, reaching forward, conquering the darkness, until it touched something that seemed more solid than a cloud.

The boy stood up. "What is that out there?" he called. "What does it rest on, out at that other end?"

In the morning sunshine a precipice shone forth beyond the gulf. A precipice – or was it a castle? The horses moved. They set their feet upon the rainbow.

"Oh, look!" the boy shouted. "Oh – listen! Those caves – or are they gateways? Oh, look between those cliffs at those ledges. I see people! I see trees!"

"Look also below," whispered Sir Thomas. "Neglect not the diviner Acheron."

The boy looked below, past the flames of the rainbow that licked against their wheels. The gulf also had cleared, and in its depths there flowed an everlasting river. One sunbeam entered and struck a green pool. and as they passed over he saw three maidens rise to the surface of the pool, singing, and playing with something that glistened like a ring.

"You down in the water –" he called.

They answered, "You up on the bridge –" There was a burst of music. "You up on the bridge, good luck to you. Truth in the depth – truth on the height."

"You down in the water, what are you doing?"

Sir Thomas Browne replied: "They sport in the mancipiary possession of their gold"; and the omnibus arrived.

The boy was in disgrace. He sat locked up in the nursery of Agathox Lodge, learning poetry for a punishment. His father had said, "My boy! I can pardon anything but untruthfulness," and had caned him, saying at each stroke, "There is no onmibus, no driver, no bridge, no mountain; you are a truant, a guttersnipe, a liar." His father could be very stern at times. His mother had begged him to say he was sorry. But he could not say that. It was the greatest day of his life, in spite of the caning and the poetry at the end or it.

He had returned punctually at sunset – driven not by Sir Thomas Browne, but by a maiden lady who was full of quiet fun. They had talked of omnibuses and also of barouche landaus. How far away her gentle voice seemed now! Yet it was scarcely three hours since he had left her up the alley.

His mother called through the door. "Dear, you are to come down and to bring your poetry with you."

He came down, and found that Mr. Bons was in the smoking-room with his father. It had been a dinner party.

"Here is the great traveler!" said his father grimly. "Here is the young gentleman who drives in an onmibus over rainbows, while young ladies sing to him." Pleased with his wit, he laughed.

"After all –" said Mr. Bons, smiling, "there is something a little like it in Wagner. It is odd how, in quite illiterate minds, you will find glimmers of Artistic Truth. The case interests me. Let me plead for the culprit. We have all romanced in our time, haven't we?"

"Hear how kind Mr. Bons is," said his mother, while his father said. "Very well. Let him say his poem – and that will do. He is going away to my sister on Tuesday, and she will cure him of this alley-slopering." (Laughter.) "Say your poem."

The boy began. "Standing aloof in giant ignorance."

His father laughed again – roared. "One for you, my son! 'Standing aloof in giant ignorance!' I never knew these poets talked sense. Just describes you. Here, Bons, you go in for poetry. Put him through it, will you, while I fetch up the whisky?"

"Yes, give me the Keats," said Mr. Bons. "Let him say his Keats to me."

So for a few moments the wise man and the ignorant boy were left alone in the smoking-room.

"'Standing aloof in giant ignorance, of thee I dream and of the Cyclades, as one who sits ashore and longs perchance to visit –'"

"Quite right. To visit what?"

"'To visit dolphin coral in deep seas,'" said the boy, and burst into tears.

"Come, come! why do you cry?"

"Because – because all these words that only rhymed before – now that I've come back they're me."

Mr. Bons laid the Keats down. The case was more interesting than he had expected. "You!" he exclaimed. "This sonnet you?"

"Yes – and look further on: 'Aye, on the shores of darkness there is light, and precipices show untrodden green.' It is so, sir. All these things are true."

"I never doubted it," said Mr. Bons, with closed eyes.

"You – then you believe me? You believe in the omnibus and the driver and the storm and that return ticket I got for nothing and –"

"Tut, tut! No more of your yarns – my boy. I meant that I never doubted the essential truth of poetry. Some day, when you have read more, you will understand what I mean."

"But Mr. Bons, it is so. There is light upon the shores of darkness. I have seen it coming. Light and a wind."

"Nonsense –" said Mr. Bons.

"If I had stopped! They tempted me. They told me to give up my ticket – for you cannot come back if you lose your ticket. They called from the river for it, and indeed I was tempted, for I have never been so happy as among those precipices. But I thought of my mother and father, and that I must fetch them. Yet they will not come, though the road starts opposite our house. It has all happened as the people up there warned me, and Mr. Bons has disbelieved me like every one else. I have been caned. I shall never see that mountain again."

"What's that about me?" said Mr. Bons – sitting up in his chair very suddenly.

"I told them about you, and how clever you were, and how many books you had – and they said, "Mr. Bons will certainly disbelieve you."

"Stuff and nonsense, my young friend. You grow impertinent. I – well – I will settle the matter. Not a word to your father. I will cure you. Tomorrow evening I will myself call here to take you for a walk, and at sunset we will go up this alley opposite and hunt for your onmibus, you silly little boy."

His face grew serious, for the boy was not disconcerted, but leapt about the room singing, "Joy! joy! I told them you would believe me. We will drive together over the rainbow. I told them that you would come." After all – could there be anything in the story? Wagner? Keats? Shelley? Sir Thomas Browne? Certainly the case was interesting.

And on the morrow evening, though it was pouring with rain, Mr. Bons did not omit to call at Agathox Lodge.

The boy was ready, bubbling with excitement, and skipping about in a way that rather vexed the President of the Literary Society. They took a turn down Buckingham Park Road, and then – having seen that no one was watching them – slipped up the alley. Naturally enough (for the sun was setting) they ran straight against the omnibus.

"Good heavens!" exclaimed Mr. Bons. "Good gracious heavens!"

It was not the omnibus in which the boy had driven first, nor yet that in which he had returned.

There were three horses – black- gray, and white, the gray being the finest. The driver, who turned round at the mention of goodness and of heaven, was a sallow man with terrifying jaws and sunken eyes. Mr. Bons, on seeing him, gave a cry as if of recognition, and began to tremble violently.

The boy jumped in.

"Is it possible?" cried Mr. Bons. "Is the impossible possible?"

"Sir; come in, sir. It is such a fine omnibus. Oh, here is his name – Dan someone.

Mr. Bons sprang in too. A blast of wind immediately slammed the omnibus door, and the shock jerked down all the omnibus blinds, which were very weak on their springs.

"Dan … Show me. Good gracious heavens! we're moving."

"Hooray!" said the boy.

Mr. Bons became flustered. He had not intended to be kidnapped. He could not find the door handle, nor push up the blinds. The omnibus was quite dark, and by the time he had struck a match, night had come on outside also. They were moving rapidly.

"A strange, a memorable adventure," he said, surveying the interior of the omnibus, which was large, roomy, and constructed with extreme regularity, every part exactly answering to every other part. Over the door (the handle of which was outside) was written. *Lasciate ogni baldanza voi che entrate* – at least, that was what was written, but Mr. Bons said that it was Lashy arty something – and that baldanza was a mistake for speranza. His voice sounded as if he was in church. Meanwhile, the boy called to the cadaverous driver for two return tickets. They were handed in without a word. Mr. Bons covered his face with his hand and again trembled. "Do you know who that is!" he whispered, when the little window had shut upon them. "It is the impossible."

"Well, I don't like him as much as Sir Thomas Browne, though I shouldn't be surprised if he had even more in him."

"More in him?" He stamped irritably. "By accident you have made the greatest discovery of the century, and all you can say is that there is more in this man. Do you remember those vellum books in my library – stamped with red lilies? This – sit still. I bring you stupendous news! – this is the man who wrote them."

The boy sat quite still. "I wonder if we shall see Mrs. Gamp?" he asked – after a civil pause.

"Mrs. –?"

"Mrs. Gamp and Mrs. Harris. I like Mrs. Harris. I came upon them quite suddenly. Mrs. Gamp's bandboxes have moved over the rainbow so badly. All the bottoms have fallen out, and two of the pippins off her bedstead tumbled into the stream."

"Out there sits the man who wrote my vellum books," thundered Mr. Bons – "and you talk to me of Dickens and of Mrs. Gamp?"

"I know Mrs. Gamp so well," he apologized. "I could not help being glad to see her. I recognized her voice. She was telling Mrs. Harris about Mrs. Prig."

"Did you spend the whole day in her elevating company?"

"Oh – no. I raced. I met a man who took me out beyond to a racecourse. You run, and there are dolphins out at sea."

"Indeed. Do you remember the man's name?"

"Achilles. No; he was later. Tom Jones."

Mr. Bons sighed heavily. "Well, my lad, you have made a miserable mess of it. Think of a cultured person with your opportunities! A cultured person would have known all these characters and known what to have said to each. He would not have wasted his time with a Mrs. Gamp or a Tom Jones. The creations of Homer, of Shakespeare, and of Him who drives us now, would alone have contented him. He would not have raced. He would have asked intelligent questions."

"But, Mr. Bons." said the boy humbly, "you will be a cultured person. I told them so."

"True, true, and I beg you not to disgrace me when we arrive. No gossiping. No running. Keep close to my side, and never speak to these Immortals unless they speak to you. Yes, and give me the return tickets. You will be losing them."

The boy surrendered the tickets, but felt a little sore. After all, he had found the way to this place. It was hard first to be disbelieved and then to be lectured. Meanwhile, the rain had stopped, and moonlight crept into the onmibus through the cracks in the blinds.

"But how is there to be a rainbow?" cried the boy.

"You distract me," snapped Mr. Bons. "I wish to meditate on beauty. I wish to goodness I was with a reverent and sympathetic person.

The lad bit his lip. He made a hundred good resolutions. He would imitate Mr. Bons all the visit. He would not laugh, or run, or sing, or do any of the vulgar things that must have disgusted his new friends last time. He would be very careful to pronounce their names properly, and to remember who knew whom. Achilles did not know Tom Jones – at least, so Mr. Bons said. The Duchess of Malfi was older than Mrs. Gamp – at least, so Mr. Bons said. He would be self-conscious, reticent, and prim. He would never say he liked anyone. Yet, when the blind flew up at a chance touch of his head, all these good resolutions went to the winds, for the omnibus had reached the summit of a moonlit hill, and there was the chasm, and there, across it – stood the old precipices, dreaming, with their feet in the everlasting river. He exclaimed. "The mountains! Listen to the new time in the water! Look at the camp fires in the ravines," and Mr. Bons after a hasty glance retorted. "Water? Camp fires? Ridiculous rubbish. Hold your tongue. There is nothing at all."

Yet, under his eyes, a rainbow formed, compounded not of sunlight and storm, but of moonlight and the spray of the river. The three horses put their feet upon it. He thought it the finest rainbow he had seen, but did not dare to say so, since Mr. Bons said that nothing was there. He leant out – the window had opened – and sang the tune that rose from the sleeping waters.

"The prelude to Rhinegold," said Mr. Bons suddenly. "Who taught you these leit motifs." He, too, looked out of the window. Then he behaved very oddly. He gave a choking cry, and fell back on to the onmibus floor. He writhed and kicked. His face was green.

"Does the bridge make you dizzy?" the boy asked.

"Dizzy," gasped Mr. Bons. "I want to go back. Tell the driver."

But the driver shook his head.

"We are nearly there," said the boy. "They are asleep. Shall I call? They will be so pleased to see you, for I have prepared them."

Mr. Bons moaned. They moved over the lunar rainbows which ever and ever broke away behind their wheels. How still the night was! Who would be sentry at the Gate?

"I am coming," he shouted, again forgetting the hundred resolutions. "I am returning – I, the boy."

"The boy is returning." cried a voice to other voices – who repeated, "The boy is returning."

"I am bringing Mr. Bons with me."

Silence.

"I should have said Mr. Bons is bringing me with him."

Profound silence.

"Who stands sentry?"

"Achilles."

And on the rocky causeway – close to the springing of the rainbow bridge, he saw a young man who carried a wonderful shield.

"Mr. Bons, it is Achilles, armed."

"I want to go back," said Mr. Bons.

The last fragment of the rainbow melted, the wheels sang upon the living rock, the door of the omnibus burst open. Out leapt the boy – he could not resist – and sprang to meet the warrior, who, stooping suddenly – caught him on his shield.

"Achilles!" he cried – "let me get down. for I am ignorant and vulgar – and I must wait for that Mr. Bons of whom I told you yesterday."

But Achilles raised him aloft. He crouched on the wonderful shield, on heroes and burning cities, on vineyards graven in gold, on every dear passion, every joy, on the entire image of the Mountain that he had discovered, encircled, like it, with an everlasting stream. "No, no" he protested. "I am not worthy. It is Mr. Bons who must be up here."

But Mr. Bons was whimpering, and Achilles trumpeted and cried, "Stand upright upon my shield!"

"Sir, I did not mean to stand! something made me stand. Sir, why do you delay? Here is only the great Achilles, whom you knew."

Mr. Bons screamed, "I see no one. I see nothing. I want to go back." Then he cried to the driver. "Save me! Let me stop in your chariot. I have honored you. I have quoted you. I have bound you in vellum. Take me back to my world."

The driver replied. "I am the means and not the end. I am the food and not the life. Stand by yourself, as that boy has stood. I cannot save you. For poetry is a spirit; and they that would worship it must worship in spirit and in truth."

Mr. Bons – he could not resist – crawled out of the beautiful omnibus. His face appeared, gaping horribly. His hands followed, one gripping the step. the other beating the air. Now his shoulders emerged, his chest, his stomach. With a shriek of "I see London." he fell – fell against the hard, moonlit rock, fell into it as if it were water, fell through it, vanished, and was seen by the boy no more.

"Where have you fallen to, Mr. Bons? Here is a procession arriving to honor you with music and torches. Here come the men and women whose names you know." The mountain is awake, the river is awake, over the race course the sea is awaking those dolphins, and it is all for you. They want you –"

There was the touch of fresh leaves on his forehead. Someone had crowned him.

ΤΕΛΟΣ

From the Kingston Gazette, Surbiton Times, and Raynes Park Observer

The body of Mr. Septimus Bons has been found in a shockingly mutilated condition in the vicinity of the Bermondsey gas works. The deceased's pockets contained a sovereign-purse, a silver cigar-case, a bijou pronouncing dictionary, and a couple of omnibus tickets. The unfortunate gentleman had apparently been hurled from a considerable height. Foul play is suspected, and a thorough investigation is pending by the authorities.

Other Kingdom

"'*Quem*, whom; *fugis*, are you avoiding; *ah demens*, you silly ass; *habitarunt di quoque*, gods too have lived in; *silvas*, the woods.' Go ahead!"

I always brighten the classics – it is part of my system – and therefore I translated demens by "silly ass." But Miss Beaumont need not have made a note of the translation, and Ford, who knows better, need not have echoed after me. "Whom are you avoiding, you silly ass, gods too have lived in the woods."

" Ye–es," I replied, with scholarly hesitation. " Ye–es. *Silvas* – woods, wooded spaces, the country generally. Yes. *Demens*, of course, is *de–mens*. Ah, witless fellow! Gods, I say, even gods have dwelt in the woods ere now."

"But I thought gods always lived in the sky," said Mrs. Worters, interrupting our lesson for I think the third-and-twentieth time.

"Not always," answered Miss Beaumont. As she spoke, she inserted "witless fellow" as an alternative to "silly ass."

"I always thought they lived in the sky."

"Oh, no, Mrs. Worters," the girl repeated. "Not always." And finding her place in the notebook she read as follows: "Gods. Where. Chief deities – Mount Olympus. Pan – most places, as name implies. Oreads – mountains, Sirens, Tritons, Nereids – water (salt). Naiads – water (fresh). Satyrs, Fauns, etc. – woods. Dryads – trees."

"Well, dear, you have learnt a lot. And will you tell me what good it has done you?"

"It has helped me –" faltered Miss Beaumont. She was very earnest over her classics. She wished she could have said what good they had done her.

Ford came to her rescue. "Of course it's helped you. The classics are full of tips. They teach you how to dodge things."

I begged my young friend not to dodge his Virgil lesson.

"But they do!" he cried. "Suppose that long-haired brute Apollo wants to give you a music lesson. Well, out you pop into the laurels. Or Universal Nature comes along. You aren't feeling particularly keen on Universal Nature, so you turn into a reed."

"Is Jack mad?" asked Mrs. Worters.

But Miss Beaumont had caught the allusions – which were quite ingenious I must admit. "And Croesus?" she inquired. "What was it one turned into to get away from Croesus?"

I hastened to tidy up her mythology. "Midas, Miss Beaumont, not Croesus. And he turns you – you don't turn yourself: he turns you into gold."

"There's no dodging Midas," said Ford.

"Surely –" said Miss Beaumont. She had been learning Latin not quite a fortnight, but she would have corrected the Regius Professor.

He began to tease her. "Oh, there's no dodging Midas! He just comes, he touches you, and you pay him several thousand percent, at once. You're gold – a young golden lady – if he touches you."

"I won't be touched!" she cried, relapsing into her habitual frivolity.

"Oh, but he'll touch you."

"He shan't!"

"He will."

"He shan't!"

"He will."

Miss Beaumont took up her Virgil and smacked Ford over the head with it.

"Evelyn! Evelyn!" said Mrs. Worters. "Now you are forgetting yourself. And you also forget my question. What good has Latin done you?"

"Mr. Inksip – what good has Latin done us?"

So I was let in for the classical controversy. The arguments for the study of Latin are perfectly sound, but they are difficult to remember, and the afternoon sun was hot, and I needed my tea. But I had to justify my existence as a coach, so I took off my eye-glasses and breathed on them and said, "My dear Ford, what a question!"

"It's all right for Jack," said Mrs. Worters, "Jack has to pass his entrance examination. But what's the good of it for Evelyn? None at all."

"No, Mrs. Worters," I persisted, pointing my eye-glasses at her. "I cannot agree. Miss Beaumont is – in a sense – new to our civilization. She is entering it, and Latin is one of the subjects in her entrance examination also. No one can grasp modern life without some knowledge of its origins."

"But why should she grasp modern life?" said the tiresome woman.

"Well, there you are!" I retorted, and shut up my eye-glasses with a snap.

"Mr. Inskip, I am not there. Kindly tell me what's the good of it all. Oh, I've been

through it myself: Jupiter, Venus, Juno, I know the lot of them. And many of the stories not at all proper."

"Classical education," I said dryly, "is not entirely confined to classical mythology. Though even the mythology has its value. Dreams if you like, but there is value in dreams."

"I too have dreams," said Mrs. Worters, "but I am not so foolish as to mention them afterwards."

Mercifully we were interrupted. A rich virile voice close behind us said, "Cherish your dreams!" We had been joined by our host, Harcourt Worters – Mrs. Worter's son,

Miss Beaumont's fiancé, Ford's guardian, my employer: I must speak of him as Mr. Worters.

"Let us cherish our dreams!" he repeated. "All day I've been fighting, haggling, bargaining. And to come out on to this lawn and see you all learning Latin, so happy, so passionless, so Arcadian –"

He did not finish the sentence, but sank into the chair next to Miss Beaumont, and possessed himself of her hand. As he did so she sang: "Ah you silly ass, gods live in woods!"

"What have we here?" said Mr. Worters with a slight frown.

With the other hand she pointed to me.

"Virgil –" I stammered. "Colloquial translation –"

"Oh, I see; a colloquial translation of poetry." Then his smile returned. "Perhaps if gods live in woods, that is why woods are so dear. I have just bought Other Kingdom Copse!"

Loud exclamations of joy. Indeed, the beeches in that copse are fine as any in Hertfordshire. Moreover, it, and the meadow by which it is approached, have always made an ugly notch in the rounded contours of the estate. So we were all very glad that

Mr. Worters had purchased Other Kingdom. Only Ford kept silent, stroking his head where the Virgil had hit it, and smiling a little to himself as he did so.

"Judging from the price I paid, I should say there was a god in every tree. But price, this time there was no object." He glanced at Miss Beaumont. "You admire beeches, Evelyn, do you not?"

"I forget always which they are. Like this?"

She flung her arms up above her head, close together, so that she looked like a slender column. Then her body swayed and her delicate green dress quivered over it with the suggestion of countless leaves.

"My dear child!" exclaimed her lover.

"No: that is a silver birch," said Ford.

"Oh, of course. Like this, then." And she twitched up her skirts so that for a moment they spread out in great horizontal layers, like the layers of a beech.

We glanced at the house, but none of the servants were looking. So we laughed, and said she ought to go on the variety stage.

"Ah, this is the kind I like!" she cried, and practiced the beech-tree again.

"I thought so," said Mr. Worters. "I thought so. Other Kingdom Copse is yours."

"Mine?" She had never had such a present in her life. She could not realize it.

"The purchase will be drawn up in your name. You will sign the deed. Receive the wood, with my love. It is a second engagement ring."

"But is it – is it mine? Can I – do what I like there?"

"You can," said Mr. Worters, smiling.

She rushed at him and kissed him. She kissed Mrs. Worters. She would have kissed myself and Ford if we had not extruded elbows. The joy of possession had turned her head.

"It's mine! I can walk there, work there, live there. A wood of my own! Mine for ever."

"Yours, at all events, for ninety-nine years."

"Ninety-nine years?" I regret to say there was a tinge of disappointment in her voice.

"My dear child! Do you expect to live longer?"

"I suppose I can't," she replied, and flushed a little. "I don't know."

"Ninety-nine seems long enough to most people. I have got this house, and the very lawn you are standing on, on a lease of ninety-nine years. Yet I call them my own, and I think I am justified. Am I not?"

"Oh, yes."

"Ninety-nine years is practically for ever. Isn't it?"

"Oh, It must be."

Ford possesses a most inflammatory notebook. Outside it is labeled "Private," inside it is headed "Practically a book." I saw him make an entry in it now, "Eternity: practically ninety-nine years."

Mr. Worters, as if speaking to himself, now observed: "My goodness! My goodness! How land has risen! Perfectly astounding."

I saw that he was in need of a Boswell, so I said: "Has it, indeed?"

"My dear Inskip. Guess what I could have got that wood for ten years ago! But I refused. Guess why."

We could not guess why.

"Because the transaction would not have been straight." A most becoming blush spread over his face as he uttered the noble word. "Not straight. Straight legally. But not morally straight. We were to force the hands of the man who owned it. I refused. The others – decent fellows in their way – told me I was squeamish. I said, 'Yes. Perhaps I am. My name is plain Harcourt Worters – not a well-known name if you go outside the City and my own country, but a name which, where it is known, carries, I flatter myself, some weight. And I will not sign my name to this. That is all. Call me squeamish if you like. But I will not sign. It is just a fad of mine. Let us call it a fad.'" He blushed again. Ford believes that his guardian blushes all over – that if you could strip him and make him talk nobly he would look like a boiled lobster. There is a picture of him in this condition in the notebook.

"So the man who owned it then didn't own it now?" said Miss Beaumont, who had followed the narrative with some interest.

"Oh, no!" said Mr. Worters.

"Why no!" said Mrs. Worters absently, as she hunted in the grass for her knitting- needle. "Of course not. It belongs to the widow."

"Tea!" cried her son, springing vivaciously to his feet. "I see tea and I want it. Come along, Evelyn. I can tell you it's no joke, a hard day in the battle of life. For life is practically a battle. To all intents and purposes a battle. Except for a few lucky fellows who can read books, and so avoid the realities. But I –"

His voice died away as he escorted the two ladies over the smooth lawn and up the stone steps to the terrace, on which the footman was placing tables and little chairs and a silver kettle-stand. More ladies came out of the house. We could just hear their shouts of excitement as they also were told of the purchase of Other Kingdom.

I like Ford. The boy has the makings of a scholar and – though for some reason he objects to the word – of a gentleman. It amused me now to see his lip curl with the vague cynicism of youth. He cannot understand the footman and the solid silver kettle-stand. They make him cross. For he has dreams – not exactly spiritual dreams: Mr. Worters is the man for those – but dreams of the tangible and the actual: robust dreams, which take him, not to heaven, but to another earth. There are no footmen in this other earth, and the kettle-stands, I suppose, will not be made of silver, and I know that everything is to be itself, and not practically something else. But what this means, and, if it means anything, what the good of it is, I am not prepared to say. For though I have just said "there is value in dreams," I only said it to silence old Mrs. Worters.

"Go ahead, man! We can't have tea till we've got through something."

He turned his chair away from the terrace, so that he could sit looking at the meadows and at the stream that runs through the meadows, and at the beech-trees of Other Kingdom that rise beyond the stream. Then, most gravely and admirably, he began to construe the Eclogues of Virgil.

II.

Other Kingdom Copse is like any other beech copse, and I am then spared the fatigue of describing it. And the stream in front of it, like many other streams, is not crossed by a bridge in the right place, and you must either walk round a mile or else you must paddle. Miss Beaumont suggested that we should paddle.

Mr. Worters accepted the suggestion tumultuously. It only became evident gradually that he was not going to adopt it.

"What fun! what fun! We will paddle to your kingdom. If only – if only it wasn't for the tea-things."

"But you can carry the tea-things on your back."

"Why yes! so I can. Or the servants could."

"Harcourt – no servants. This is my picnic, and my wood. I'm going to settle everything. I didn't tell you: I've got all the food. I've been in the village with Mr. Ford."

"In the village?"

"Yes. We got biscuits and oranges and half a pound of tea. That's all you'll have. He carried them up. And he'll carry them over the stream. I want you just to lend me some tea-things – not the best ones. I'll take care of them. That's all."

"Dear creature … "

"Evelyn," said Mrs. Worters, "how much did you and Jack pay for that tea?"

"For the half-pound, ten pence."

Mrs. Worters received the announcement in gloomy silence.

"Mother!" cried Mr. Worters. "Why, I forgot! How could we go paddling with mother?"

"Oh, but, Mrs. Worters, we could carry you over."

"Thank you, dearest child. I am sure you could."

"Alas! alas! Evelyn. Mother is laughing at us. She would sooner die than be carried. And alas! there are my sisters, and Mrs. Osgood: she has a cold, tiresome woman. No: we shall have to go round by the bridge."

"But some of us " began Ford. His guardian cut him short with a quick look.

So we went round – a procession of eight. Miss Beaumont led us. She was full of fun – at least I thought at the time, but when I reviewed her speeches afterwards I could not find in them anything amusing. It was all this kind of thing: "Single file! Pretend you're in church and don't talk. Mr. Ford, turn out your toes. Harcourt – at the bridge throw to the Naiad a pinch of tea. She has a headache. She has had a headache for nineteen hundred years." All that she said was quite stupid. I cannot think why I liked it at the time.

As we approached the copse she said, "Mr. Inskip, sing , and we'll sing after you: Ah you silly ass gods live in woods." I cleared my throat and gave out the abominable phrase, and we all chanted it as if it were a litany. There was something attractive about Miss Beaumont. I was not surprised that Harcourt had picked her out of "Ireland" and had brought her home, without money, without connections, almost without antecedents, to be his bride. It was daring of him, but he knew himself to be a daring fellow. She brought him nothing; but that he could afford, he had so vast a surplus of spiritual and commercial goods. "In time," I heard him tell his mother, "in time Evelyn will repay me a thousandfold." Meanwhile there was something attractive about her. If it were my place to like people, I could have liked her very much.

"Stop singing!" she cried. We had entered the wood. "Welcome, all of you." We bowed. Ford, who had not been laughing, bowed down to the ground. "And now be seated. Mrs. Worters – will you sit there – against that tree with a green trunk? It will show up your beautiful dress."

"Very well, dear, I will," said Mrs. Worters.

"Anna – there. Mr. Inskip next to her. Then Ruth and Mrs. Osgood. Oh, Harcourt – do sit a little forward, so that you'll hide the house. I don't want to see the house at all."

"I won't!" laughed her lover, "I want my back against a tree, too."

"Miss Beaumont," asked Ford, "where shall I sit?" He was standing at attention, like a soldier.

"Oh, look at all these Worters!" she cried, "and one little Ford in the middle of them!" For she was at that state of civilization which appreciates a pun.

"Shall I stand, Miss Beaumont? Shall I hide the house from you if I stand?"

"Sit down, Jack, you baby!" cried his guardian, breaking in with needless asperity. "Sit down!"

"He may just as well stand if he will," said she. "Just pull back your soft hat, Mr. Ford. Like a halo. Now you hide even the smoke from the chimneys. And it makes you beautiful."

"Evelyn! Evelyn! You are too hard on the boys. You'll tire him. He's one of those bookworms. He's not strong. Let him sit down."

"Aren't you strong?" she asked.

"I am strong!" he cried. It is quite true. Ford has no right to be strong, but he is. He never did his dumb-bells or played in his school fifteen. But the muscles came. He thinks they came while he was reading Pindar.

"Then you may just as well stand, if you will."

"Evelyn! Evelyn! childish, selfish maiden! If poor Jack gets tired I will take his place. Why don't you want to see the house! Eh?"

Mrs. Worter and the Miss Worters moved uneasily. They saw that their Harcourt was not quite pleased. Theirs not to question why. It was for Evelyn to remove his displeasure, and they glanced at her.

"Well, why don't you want to see your future home? I must say – though I practically planned the house myself – that it looks very well from here. I like the gables. Miss! Answer me!"

I felt for Miss Beaumont. A home-made gable is an awful thing, and Harcourt's mansion looked like a cottage with the dropsy. But what would she say?

She said nothing.

"Well?"

It was as if he had never spoken. She was as merry, as smiling, as pretty as ever, and she said nothing. She had not realized that a question requires an answer.

For us the situation was intolerable. I had to save it by making a tactful reference to the view, which, I said, reminded me a little of the country near Veii. It did not – indeed it could not, for I have never been near Veii. But it is part of my system to make classical allusions. And at all events I saved the situation.

Miss Beaumont was serious and rational at once. She asked me the date of Veii. I made a suitable answer.

"I do like the classics," she informed us. "They are so natural. Just writing down things."

"Ye–es, said I. "But the classics have their poetry as well as their prose. They're more than a record of facts."

"Just writing down things," said Miss Beaumont, and smiled as if the silly definition pleased her.

Harcourt had recovered himself. "A very just criticism," said he. "It is what I always feel about the ancient world. It takes us but a very little way. It only writes things down."

"What do you mean?" asked Evelyn.

"I mean this – though it is presumptuous to speak in the presence of Mr. Inskip. This is what I mean. The classics are not everything. We owe them an enormous debt; I am the last to undervalue it; I, too, went through them at school. They are full of elegance and beauty. But they are not everything. They were written before men began to really feel." He colored crimson. "Hence, the chilliness of classical art – its lack of– of a something. Whereas later things – Dante – a Madonna of Raphael – some bars of Mendelssohn –" His voice tailed reverently away. We sat with our eyes on the ground, not liking to look at Miss Beaumont. It is a fairly open secret that she also lacks a something. She has not yet developed her soul.

The silence was broken by the still small voice of Mrs. Worters saying that she was faint with hunger.

The young hostess sprang up. She would let none of us help her: it was her party. She undid the basket and emptied out the biscuits and oranges from their bags, and boiled the kettle and poured out the tea, which was horrible. But we laughed and talked with the frivolity that suits the open air, and even Mrs. Worters expectorated her flies with a smile. Over us all there stood the silent, chivalrous figure of Ford, drinking tea carefully lest it should disturb his outline. His guardian, who is a wag, chaffed him and tickled his ankles and calves.

"Well, this is nice!" said Miss Beaumont. "I am happy."

"Your wood, Evelyn!" said the ladies.

"Her wood for ever!" cried Mr. Worters. "It is an unsatisfactory arrangement, a ninety-nine years' lease. There is no feeling of permanency. I reopened negotiations. I have bought her the wood for ever – all right, dear, all right: don't make a fuss."

"But I must!" she cried, "For everything's perfect! Everyone's so kind – and I didn't know most of you a year ago. Oh, it is so wonderful – and now a wood – a wood of my own – a wood for ever. All of you coming to tea with me here! Dear Harcourt – dear people – and just where the house would come and spoil things, there is Mr. Ford!"

"Ha! ha!" laughed Mr. Worters, and slipped his hand up round the boy's ankle. What happened I did not know, but Ford collapsed on to the ground with a sharp cry. To an outsider it might have sounded like a cry of anger or pain. We, who knew better, laughed uproariously.

"Down he goes! Down he goes!" And they struggled playfully, kicking up the mould and the dry leaves.

"Don't hurt my wood!" cried Miss Beaumont.

Ford gave another sharp cry. Mr. Worters withdrew his hand. "Victory!" he exclaimed. "Evelyn! behold the family seat!" But Miss Beaumont, in her butterfly fashion, had left us, and was strolling away into her wood.

We packed up the tea-things and then split into groups. Ford went with the ladies. Mr. Worters did me the honor to stop by me.

"Well!" he said, in accordance with his usual formula, "and how go the classics?"

"Fairly well."

"Does Miss Beaumont show any ability?"

"I should say that she does. At all events she has enthusiasm."

"You do not think it is the enthusiasm of a child? I will be frank with you, Mr. Inskip. In many ways Miss Beaumont's practically a child. She has everything to learn: she acknowledges as much herself. Her new life is so different – so strange. Our habits – our thoughts – she has to be initiated into them all."

I saw what he was driving at, but I am not a fool, and I replied: "And how can she be initiated better than through the classics?"

"Exactly, exactly," said Mr. Worters. In the distance we heard her voice. She was counting the beech-trees. "The only question is – this Latin and Greek – what will she do with it? Can she make anything of it? Can she – well, it's not as if she will ever have to teach it to others."

"That is true." And my features might have been observed to become undecided.

"Whether, since she knows so little – I grant you she has enthusiasm, but ought one to divert her enthusiasm – say to English literature? She scarcely knows her Tennyson at all. Last night in the observatory I read her that wonderful scene between Arthur and

Guinevere. Greek and Latin are all very well, but I sometimes feel we ought to begin at the beginning."

"You feel," said I, "that for Miss Beaumont the classics are something of a luxury."

"A luxury. That is the exact word, Mr. Inskip. A luxury. A whim. It is all very well for Jack Ford. And here we come to another point. Surely she keeps Jack back?

Her knowledge must be elementary."

"Well, her knowledge is elementary: and I must say that it's difficult to teach them together. Jack has read a good deal, one way and another, whereas Miss Beaumont, though diligent and enthusiastic –"

"So I have been feeling. The arrangement is scarcely fair on Jack?"

"Well, I must admit –"

"Quite. I ought never to have suggested it. It must come to an end. Of course, Mr.

Inskip, it shall make no difference to you, this withdrawal of a pupil."

"The lessons shall cease at once, Mr. Worters."

Here she came up to us. "Harcourt, there are seventy-eight trees. I have had such a

count."

He smiled down at her. Let me remember to say that he is tall and handsome, with a strong chin and liquid brown eyes, and a high forehead and hair not at all gray. Few things are more striking than a photograph of Mr. Harcourt Worters.

"Seventy-eight trees?"

"Seventy-eight."

"Are you pleased?"

"Oh, Harcourt –!"

I began to pack up the tea-things. They both saw and heard me. It was their own fault if they did not go further.

"I'm looking forward to the bridge," said he. "A rustic bridge at the bottom, and then, perhaps, an asphalt path from the house over the meadow, so that in all weathers we can walk here dry-shod. The boys come into the wood – look at all these initials – and I thought of putting a simple fence, to prevent anyone but ourselves– "

"Harcourt!"

"A simple fence," he continued, "just like what I have put round my garden and the fields. Then at the other side of the copse, away from the house, I would put a gate, and have keys – two keys, I think – one for me and one for you – not more; and I would bring the asphalt path–"

"But Harcourt –"

"But Evelyn!"

"I – I – I –"

"You – you – you?"

"I – I don't want an asphalt path."

"No? Perhaps you are right. Cinders perhaps. Yes. Or even gravel."

"But Harcourt – I don't want a path at all. I – I – can't afford a path."

He gave a roar of triumphant laughter. "Dearest! As if you were going to be bothered! The path's part of my present."

"The wood is your present," said Miss Beaumont. "Do you know – I don't care for the path. I'd rather always come as we came today. And I don't want a bridge. No –nor a fence either. I don't mind the boys and their initials. They and the girls have always come up to Other Kingdom and cut their names together in the bark. It's called the Fourth Time of Asking. I don't want it to stop."

"Ugh!" He pointed to a large heart transfixed by an arrow. "Ugh! Ugh!" I suspect that he was gaining time.

"They cut their names and go away, and when the first child is born they come again and deepen the cuts. So for each child. That's how you know: the initials that go right through to the wood are the fathers and mothers of large families, and the scratches in the bark that soon close up are boys and girls who were never married at all."

"You wonderful person! I've lived here all my life and never heard a word of this. Fancy folklore in Hertfordshire! I must tell the Archdeacon: he will be delighted –"

"And Harcourt, I don't want this to stop."

"My dear girl, the villagers will find other trees! There's nothing particular in Other Kingdom."

"But –"

"Other Kingdom shall be for us. You and I alone. Our initials only." His voice sank to a whisper.

"I don't want it fenced in." Her face was turned to me; I saw that it was puzzled and frightened. "I hate fences. And bridges. And all paths. It is my wood. Please: you gave me the wood."

"Why, yes!" he replied, soothing her. But I could see that he was angry. "Of course. But aha! Evelyn, the meadow's mine; I have a right to fence there – between my domain and yours!"

"Oh, fence me out if you like! Fence me out as much as you like! But never in. Oh, Harcourt, never in. I must be on the outside, I must be where anyone can reach me. Year by year – while the initials deepen – the only thing worth feeling – and at last they close up – but one has felt them."

"Our initials!" he murmured, seizing upon the one word which he had understood and which was useful to him. "Let us carve our initials now. You and I – a heart if you like it, and an arrow and everything. H.W.–E.B."

"H.W.," she repeated, "and E.B."

He took out his penknife and drew her away in search of an unsullied tree. "E. B., Eternal Blessing. Mine! Mine! My haven from the world! My temple of purity. Oh, the spiritual exaltation – you cannot understand it, but you will! Oh, the seclusion of Paradise. Year after year alone together, all in all to each other – year after year, soul to soul, E. B., Everlasting Bliss!"

He stretched out his hand to cut the initials. As he did so she seemed to awake from a dream. "Harcourt!' she cried, "Harcourt! What's that? What's that red stuff on your finger and thumb?"

III.

Oh, my goodness! Oh, all ye goddesses and gods! Here's a mess. Mr. Worters has been reading Ford's inflammatory notebook.

"It is my own fault," said Ford. "I should have labeled it 'Practically Private.' How

could he know he was not meant to look inside?"

I spoke out severely, as an employé should. "My dear boy, none of that. The label came unstuck. That was why Mr. Worters opened the book. He never suspected it was private. See – the label's off."

"Scratched off," Ford retorted grimly, and glanced at his ankle.

I affected not to understand. "The point is this. Mr. Worters is thinking the matter over for four-and-twenty hours. If you take my advice you will apologize before that time elapses."

"And if I don't?"

"You know your own affairs of course. But don't forget that you are young and practically ignorant of life, and that you have scarcely any money of your own. As far as I can see, your career practically depends on the favor of Mr. Worters. You have laughed at him. He does not like being laughed at. It seems to me that your course is obvious."

"Apology?"

"Complete."

"And if I don't?"

"Departure."

He sat down on the stone steps and rested his head on his knees. On the lawn below us was Miss Beaumont, draggling about with some croquet balls. Her lover was out in the meadow, superintending the course of the asphalt path. For the path is to me bade, and so is the bridge, and the fence is to be built round Other Kingdom after all. In time Miss Beaumont saw how unreasonable were her objections. Of her own accord, one evening in the drawing-room, she gave her Harcourt permission to do what he liked. "That wood looks nearer," said Ford.

"The inside fences have gone: that brings it nearer. But my dear boy – you must settle what you're going to do."

"How much has he read?"

"Naturally he only opened the book. From what you showed me of it, one glance would be enough."

"Did he open at the poems?"

"Poems?"

"Did he speak of the poems?"

"No. Were they about him?"

"They were not about him."

"Then it wouldn't matter if he saw them."

"It is sometimes a compliment to be mentioned," said Ford, looking up at me. The remark had a stinging fragrance about it – such a fragrance as clings to the mouth after admirable wine. It did not taste like the remark of a boy. I was sorry that my pupil was likely to wreck his career; and I told him again that he had better apologize.

"I won't speak of Mr. Worters' claim for an apology. That's an aspect on which I prefer not to couth. The point is, if you don't apologize, you go – where?"

"To an aunt at Peckham."

"I pointed to the pleasant, comfortable landscape, full of cows and carriage-horses out at grass, and civil retainers. In the midst of it stood Mr. Worters, radiating energy and wealth, like a terrestrial sun. "My dear Ford – don't be heroic! Apologize."

Unfortunately I raised my voice a little, and Miss Beaumont heard me, down on the lawn.

"Apologize?" she cried. "What about?" And as she was not interested in the game, she came up the steps towards us, trailing her croquet mallet behind her. Her walk was rather listless. She was toning down at last

"Come indoors!" I whispered. "We must get out of this."

"Not a bit of it!" said Ford.

"What is it?" she asked, standing beside him on the step.

He swallowed something as he looked up at her. Suddenly I understood. I knew the nature and the subject of his poems. I was not so sure now that he had better apologize. The sooner he was kicked out of the place the better.

In spite of my remonstrances, he told her about the book, and her first remark was: "Oh, do let me see it!" She had no "proper feeling" of any kind. Then she said: "But why do you both look so sad?"

"We are awaiting Mr. Worters' decision," said I.

"Mr. Inskip! What nonsense! Do you suppose Harcourt'll be angry?"

"Of course he is angry, and rightly so."

"But why?"

"Ford has laughed at him."

"But what's that!" And for the first time there was anger in her voice. "Do you mean to say he'll punish someone who laughs at him? Why, for what else – for whatever reason are we all here? Not to laugh at each other! I laugh at people all day. At Mr. Ford. At you. And so does Harcourt. Oh, you've misjudged him! He won't – he couldn't be angry with people who laughed."

"Mine is not nice laughter," said Ford.

"He could not well forgive me."

"You're a silly boy." She sneered at him. "You don't know Harcourt. So generous in every way. Why, he'd be as furious as I should be if you apologized. Mr. Inskip, isn't that so?"

"He has every right to an apology, I think."

"Right? What's a right? You use too many new words. 'Rights' – 'apologies' – 'society' – 'position' – I don't follow it. What are we all here for, anyhow?"

Her discourse was full of trembling lights and shadows – frivolous one moment, the next moment asking why Humanity is here. I did not take the Moral Science Tripos, so I could not tell her.

"One thing I know – and that is that Harcourt isn't as stupid as you two. He soars above conventions. He doesn't care about 'rights' and apologies. He knows that all laughter is nice, and that the other nice things are money and the soul and so on."

The soul and so on! I wonder that Harcourt out in the meadows did not have an apoplectic fit.

"Why, what a poor business your life would be," she continued, if you all kept taking offence and apologizing! Forty million people in England and all of them touchy! How one would laugh if it was true! Just imagine!" And she did laugh. "Look at Harcourt though. He know better. He isn't petty like that. Mr. Ford! He isn't petty like that. Why, what's wrong with your eyes?"

He rested his head on his knees again, and we could see his eyes no longer. In dispassionate tones she informed me that she thought he was crying. Then she tapped him on the hair with her mallet and said: "Crybaby! Crybaby! Crying about nothing!" and ran laughing down the steps. "All right!" she shouted from the lawn. "Tell the crybaby to stop. I'm going to speak to Harcourt!"

We watched her go in silence. Ford had scarcely been crying. His eyes had only become large and angry. He used such swear-words as he knew, and then got up abruptly, and went into the house. I think he could not bear to see her disillusioned. I had no such tenderness, and it was with considerable interest that I watched Miss Beaumont approach her lord.

She walked confidently across the meadow, bowing to the workmen as they raised their hats. Her languor had passed, and with it her suggestion of "tone." She was the same crude, unsophisticated person that Harcourt had picked out of Ireland – beautiful and ludicrous in the extreme, and – if you go in for pathos – extremely pathetic.

I saw them meet, and soon she was hanging on his arm. The motion of his hand explained to her the construction of bridges. Twice she interrupted him: he had to explain everything again. Then she got in her word, and what followed was a good deal better than a play.

Their two little figures parted and met and parted again, she gesticulating, he most pompous and calm. She pleaded, he argued and – if satire can carry half a mile – she tried to be satirical. To enforce one of her childish points she made two steps back. Splash! She was floundering in the little stream.

That was the dénoument of the comedy. Harcourt rescued her, while the workmen crowded round in an agitated chorus. She was wet quite as far as her knees, and muddy over her ankles. In this state she was conducted towards me, and in time I began to hear words; "Influenza – a slight immersion – clothes are of no consequence beside health – pray, dearest, don't worry – yes, it must have been a shock – bed! bed! I insist on bed! Promise? Good girl. Up the steps to bed then."

They parted on the lawn, and she came obediently up the steps. Her face was full of terror and bewilderment.

"So you've had a wetting, Miss Beaumont!"

"Wetting? Oh, yes. But, Mr. Inskip – I don't understand: I've failed."

I expressed surprise.

"Mr. Ford is to go – at once. I've failed."

"I'm sorry."

"I've failed with Harcourt. He's offended. He won't laugh. He won't let me do what I want. Latin and Greek began it: I wanted to know about gods and heroes and he wouldn't let me: then I wanted no fence round Other Kingdom and no bridge and no path – and look! Now I ask that Mr. Ford, who has done nothing, shan't be punished for it – and he is to go away forever."

"Impertinence is not 'nothing,' Miss Beaumont." For I must keep in with Harcourt.

"Impertinence is nothing!" she cried. "It doesn't exist. It's a sham, like 'claims' and 'position' and 'rights.' It's part of the great dream."

"What 'great dream'?" I asked, trying not to smile.

"Tell Mr. Ford – here comes Harcourt; I must go to bed. Give my love to Mr. Ford, and tell him 'to guess.' I shall never see him again, and I won't stand it. Tell him to guess. I am sorry I called him a crybaby. He was not crying like a baby. He was crying like a grown-up person, and now I have grown up too."

I judged it right to repeat this conversation to my employer.

IV.

The bridge is built, the fence finished, and Other Kingdom lies tethered by a ribbon of asphalt to our front door. The seventy-eight trees therein certainly seem nearer, and during the windy nights that followed Ford's departure we could hear their branches sighing, and would find in the morning that beech-leaves had been blown right up against the house. Miss Beaumont male no attempt to go out, much to the relief of the ladies, for Harcourt had given the word that she was not to go out unattended, and the boisterous weather deranged their petticoats. She remained indoors, neither reading nor laughing, and dressing no longer in green, but in brown.

Not noticing her presence, Mr. Worters looked in one day and said with a sigh of relief: "That's all right. The circle's completed."

"Is it indeed!" she replied.

"You there, you quiet little mouse? I only meant that our lords, the British workmen, have at last condescended to complete their labors and have rounded us off from the world. I – in the end I was a naughty, domineering tyrant, and disobeyed you. I didn't have the gate out at the further side of the copse. Will you forgive me? "

"Anything, Harcourt, that pleases you, is certain to please me."

The ladies smiled at each other, and Mr. Worters said: "That's right, and as soon as the wind goes down we'll all progress together to your wood, and take possession of it formally, for it didn't really count that last time."

"No, it didn't really count that last time," Miss Beaumont echoed.

"Evelyn says this wind never will go down," remarked Mrs. Worters. "I don't know how she knows."

"It will never go down, as long as I am in the house."

"Really?" he said gaily. "Then come out now, and send it down with me."

They took a few turns up and down the terrace. The wind lulled for a moment, but blew fiercer than ever during lunch. As we ate, it roared and whistled down the chimney at us, and the trees of Other Kingdom frothed like the sea. Leaves and twigs flew from them, and a bough, a good-sized bough, was blown on to the smooth asphalt path, and actually switchbacked over the bridge, up the meadow and across our very lawn. (I venture to say "our," as I am now staying on as Harcourt's secretary.) Only the stone steps prevented it from reaching the terrace and perhaps breaking the dining-room window. Miss Beaumont sprang up and, napkin in hand, ran out and touched it.

"Oh, Evelyn – " the ladies cried.

"Let her go," said Mr. Worters tolerantly. "It certainly is a remarkable incident, remarkable. We must remember to tell the Archdeacon about it."

"Harcourt," she cried, with the first hint of returning color in her cheeks,"mightn't

we go up to the copse after lunch, you and I?"

Mr. Worters considered.

"Of course, not if you don't think best."

"Inskip, what's your opinion?"

I saw what his own was, and cried, "Oh, let's go!" though I detest the wind as much as anyone.

"Very well. Mother, Anna, Ruth, Mrs. Osgood – we'll all go."

And go we did, a lugubrious procession; but the gods were good to us for once, for as soon as we were started, the tempest dropped, and there ensued an extraordinary calm. After all, Miss Beaumont was something of a weather prophet. Her spirits improved every minute. She tripped in front of us along the asphalt path, and ever and anon turned round to say to her lover some gracious or alluring thing. I admired her for it. I admire people who know on which side their bread's buttered.

"Evelyn, come here!"

"Come here yourself."

"Give me a kiss."

"Come and take it then."

He ran after her, and she ran away, while all our party laughed melodiously.

"Oh, I am so happy!" she cried. "I think I've everything I want in all the world. Oh dear, those last few days indoors! But oh, I am so happy now!" She had changed her brown dress for the old flowing green one, and she began to do her skirt dance in the open meadow, lit by sudden gleams of the sunshine. It was really a beautiful sight, and Mr. Worters did not correct her, glad perhaps that she should recover her spirits, even if she lost her tone. Her feet scarcely moved, but her body so swayed and her dress spread so gloriously around her, that we were transported with joy. She danced to the song of a bird that sang passionately in Other Kingdom, and the river held back its waves to watch her (one might have supposed), and the winds lay spell-bound in their cavern, and the great clouds spell-bound in the sky. She danced away from our society and our life, back, back, through the centuries till houses and fences fell and the earth lay wild to the sun. Her garment was as foliage upon her, the strength of her limbs as boughs, her throat the smooth upper branch that salutes the morning or glistens to the rain. Leaves move, leaves hide it as hers was hidden by the motion of her hair. Leaves move again and it is ours, as her throat was ours again when, parting the tangle, she faced us crying, "Oh!" crying, "Oh Harcourt! I never was so happy. I have all that there is in the world."

But he, untrammeled in love's ecstasy, forgetting certain Madonnas of Raphael, forgetting, I fancy, his soul, sprang to inarm her with, "Evelyn! Eternal Bliss! Mine to eternity! Mine!" and she sprang away. Music was added and she sang, "Oh Ford! oh Ford, among all these Worters, I am coming through you to my Kingdom. Oh Ford, my lover while I was a woman, I will never forget you, never, as long as I have branches to shade you from the sun," and, singing, crossed the stream.

Why he followed her so passionately, I do not know. It was play, she was in his own domain which a fence surrounds, and she could not possibly escape him. But he dashed round by the bridge as if all their love was at stake, and pursued her with fierceness up the hill. She ran well, but the end was a foregone conclusion, and we only speculated whether he would catch her outside or inside the copse. He gained on her inch by inch; now they were in the shadow of the trees; he had practically grasped her, he had missed; she had disappeared into the trees themselves, he following.

"Harcourt is in high spirits," said Mrs. Osgood, Anna, and Ruth.

"Evelyn!" we heard him shouting within.

We proceeded up the asphalt path.

"Evelyn! Evelyn!"

"He's not caught her yet, evidently."

"Where are you, Evelyn?"

"Miss Beaumont must have hidden herself rather cleverly."

"Look here," cried Harcourt, emerging, "have you seen Evelyn?"

"Oh, no, she's certainly inside."

"So I thought."

"Evelyn must be dodging round one of the trunks. You go this way, I that. We'll soon find her."

We searched, gaily at first, and always with a feeling that Miss Beaumont was close by, that the delicate limbs were just behind this bole, the hair and the drapery quivering among those leaves. She was beside us, above us; here was her footstep on the purple-brown earth – her bosom, her neck – she everywhere and nowhere. Gaiety turned to irritation, irritation to anger and fear. Miss Beaumont was apparently lost. "Evelyn! Evelyn!" we continued to cry. "Oh, really, it is beyond a joke."

Then the wind arose, the more violent for its lull, and we were driven into the house by a terrific storm. We said, "At all events she will come back now." But she did not come, and the rain hissed and rose up from the dry meadows like incense smoke, and smote the quivering leaves to applause. Then it lightened. Ladies screamed, and we saw Other Kingdom as one who claps the hands, and heard it as one who roars with laughter in the thunder. Not even the Archdeacon can remember such a storm. All Harcourt's seedlings were ruined, and the tiles flew off his gables right and left. He came to me presently with a white, drawn face, saying: "Inskip, can I trust you?"

"You can, indeed."

"I have long suspected it; she has eloped with Ford."

"But how –" I gasped.

"The carriage is ready – we'll talk as we drive." Then, against the rain he shouted: "No gate in the fence, I know, but what about a ladder? While I blunder, she's over the fence, and he –"

"But you were so close. There was not the time."

"There is time for anything," he said venomously, "where a treacherous woman is concerned. I found her no better than a savage, I trained her, I educated her. But I'll break them both. I can do that; I'll break them soul and body."

No one can break Ford now. The task is impossible. But I trembled for Miss Beaumont.

We missed the train. Young couples had gone by it, several young couples, and we heard of more young couples in London, as if all the world were mocking Harcourt's solitude. In desperation we sought the squalid suburb that is now Ford's home. We swept past the dirty maid and the terrified aunt, swept upstairs, to catch him if we could red-handed. He was seated at the table, reading the Œdipus Coloneus of Sophocles.

"That won't take in me!" shouted Harcourt. "You've got Miss Beaumont with you, and I know it."

"No such luck," said Ford.

He stammered with rage. "Inskip – you hear that? 'No such luck'! Quote the evidence against him. I can't speak."

So I quoted her song. "'Oh Ford! Oh Ford, among all these Worters, I am coming through you to my Kingdom! Oh Ford, my lover while I was a woman, I will never forget you, never, as long as I have branches to shade you from the sun.' Soon after that, we lost her."

"And – and on another occasion she sent a message of similar effect. Inskip, bear witness. He was to 'guess' something."

"I have guessed it," said Ford.

"So you practically –"

"Oh, no, Mr. Worters, you mistake me. I have not practically guessed. I have guessed. I could tell you if I chose, but it would be no good, for she has not practically escaped you. She has escaped you absolutely, forever and ever, as long as there are branches to shade men from the sun."

The Curate's Friend

It is uncertain how the Faun came to be in Wiltshire. Perhaps he came over with the Roman legionaries live with his friends in camp, talking to them of Lucretilis, or Garganus or of the slopes of Etna; they in the joy of their recall forgot to take him on board, and he wept in exile; but at last he found that our hills also understood his sorrows, and rejoiced when he was happy. Or, perhaps he came to be there because he had been there always. There is nothing particularly classical about a faun: it is only that the Greeks and Italians have ever had the sharpest eyes. You will find him in the "Tempest" and the "Benedicte" and in any country which has beech clumps and sloping grass and very clear streams may reasonably produce him

How I came to see him is a more difficult question. For to see him there is required a certain quality, for which truthfulness is too cold a name and animal spirits too coarse a one, and he alone knows how this quality came to be in me. No man has the right to call himself a fool, but I may say that I then presented the perfect semblance of one. I was facetious without humor and serious without conviction. Every Sunday I would speak to my rural parishioners about the other world in the tone of one who has been behind the scenes, or I would explain to them the errors of the Pelagians, or I would warn them against hurrying from one dissipation to another. Every Tuesday I gave what I called "straight talks to my lads" – talks which led straight past anything awkward. And every Thursday I addressed the Mothers' Union on the duties of wives or widows, and gave them practical hints on the management of a family often.

I took myself in, and for a time I certainly took in Emily. I have never known a girl attend so carefully to my sermons, or laugh so heartily at my jokes. It is no wonder that I became engaged. She has made an excellent wife, freely correcting her husband's absurdities, but allowing no one else to breathe a word against them; able to talk about the subconscious self in the drawing-room, and yet have an ear for the children crying in the nursery, or the plates breaking in the scullery. An excellent wife – better than I ever imagined. But she has not married me.

Had we stopped indoors that afternoon nothing would have happened. It was all owing tot Emily's mother, who insisted on our tea-ing out. Opposite the village, across the stream, was a small chalk down, crowned by a beech copse and a few Roman earthworks. (I lectured very vividly on those earthworks: they have since proved to be Saxon.) Hither did I drag up a tea-basket and a heavy rug for Emily's mother, while Emily and a little friend went on in front. The little friend – who has played all through a much less important part than he supposes – a pleasant youth, full of intelligence and poetry, especially of what he called the poetry of earth. He longed to wrest earth's secret from her, and I have seen him press his face passionately into the grass, even when he has believed himself to be alone. Emily was at that time full of vague aspirations, and, though I should have preferred them all to center in me, yet it seemed unreasonable to deny her such other opportunities for self-culture as the neighborhood provided.

It was then my habit, on reaching the top of any eminence, to exclaim facetiously "And who will stand on either hand and keep the bridge with me?" at the same moment violently agitating my arms or casting my wide-awake at an imaginary foe. Emily and the friend received my sally as usual, nor could I detect any insincerity in their mirth. Yet I was convinced that someone was present who did not think I had been funny, and any public speaker will understand my growing uneasiness.

I was somewhat cheered by Emily's mother, who puffed up exclaiming, "Kind Harry, to carry the things! What should we do without you, even now! Oh, what a view! Can you see the dear Cathedral? No. Too hazy. Now I'm going to sit right on the rug." She smiled mysteriously. "The downs in September, you know."

We gave some perfunctory admiration to the landscape, which is indeed only beautiful to those who admire land, and to them perhaps the most beautiful in England. For here is the body of the great chalk spider who straddles over our island – whose legs are the south downs and the north downs and the Chilterns, and the tips of whose toes poke out at Cromer and Dover. He is a clean creature, who grows as few trees as he can, and those few in tidy clumps, and he loves to be tickled by quickly flowing streams. He is pimpled all over with earthworks, for from the beginning of time men have fought for the privilege of standing on him, and the oldest of our temples is built upon his back.

But in those days I liked my country snug and pretty, full of gentlemen's residences and shady bowers and people who touch their hats. The expanses on which one may walk for miles and hardly shift a landmark or meet a genteel person were still intolerable to me. I turned away as soon as propriety allowed me and said "And may I now prepare the cup that cheers?"

Emily's mother replied: "Kind man, to help me. I always do say that tea out is worth the extra effort. I wish we led simpler lives." We agreed with her. I spread out the food. "Won't the kettle stand? Oh, but make it stand." I did so. There was a little cry, faint but distinct, as of something in pain.

"How silent it all is up here!" said Emily.

I dropped a lighted match on the grass, and again I heard the little cry.

"What is that?" I asked.

"I only said it was so silent," said Emily.

"Silent, indeed," echoed the little friend. Silent! the place was full of noises. If the match had fallen in a drawing-room it could not have been worse, and the loudest noise came from beside Emily herself. I had exactly the sensation of going to a great party, of waiting to be announced in the echoing hall, where I could hear the voices of the guests, but could not yet see their faces. It is a nervous moment for a self-conscious man, especially if all the voices should be strange to him, and he has never met his host.

"My dear Harry!" said the elder lady, "never mind about that match. That'll smolder away and harm no one. Tea-ee-ee ! I always say – and you will find Emily the same – that as the magic hour of five approaches, no matter how good a lunch, one begins to feel a sort of –"

Now the Faun is of the kind who capers upon the Neo-Attic reliefs, and if you do not notice his ears or see his tail, you take him for a man and are horrified.

"Bathing!" I cried wildly. "Such a thing for our village lads, but I quite agree – more supervision – I blame myself. Go away, bad boy, go away!"

"What will he think of next!" said Emily, while the creature beside her stood up and beckoned to me. I advanced struggling and gesticulating with tiny steps and horrified cries, exorcising the apparition with my hat. Not otherwise had I advanced the day before, when Emily's nieces showed me their guinea pigs. And by no less hearty laughter was I greeted now. Until the strange fingers closed upon me, I thought that here was one of my parishioners and did not cease to exclaim, "Let me go, naughty boy, let go!" And Emily's mother, believing herself to have detected the joke, replied, "Well I must confess they are naughty boys and reach one even on the rug: the downs in September, as I said before."

Here I caught sight of the tail, uttered a wild shriek and fled into the beech copse behind.

"Harry would have been a born actor," said Emily's mother as I left them.

I realized that a great crisis in my life was approaching, and that if I failed in it I might permanently lose my self-esteem. Already in the wood I was troubled by a multitude of voices – the voices of the hill beneath me, of the trees over my head, of the very insects in the bark of the tree. I could even hear the stream licking little pieces out of the meadows, and the meadows dreamily protesting. Above the din – which is no louder than the flight of a bee – rose the Faun's voice saying, "Dear priest, be placid, be placid: why are you frightened?"

"I am not frightened," said I – and indeed I was not." But I am grieved: you have disgraced me in the presence of ladies."

"No one else has seen me," he said, smiling idly. "The women have tight boots and the man has long hair. Those kinds never see. For years I have only spoken to children, and they lose sight of me as soon as they grow up. But you will not be able to lose sight of me, and until you die you will be my friend. Now I begin to make you happy: lie upon your back or run races, or climb trees, or shall I get you

blackberries, or harebells, or wives."

In a terrible voice I said to him, "Get thee behind me!" He got behind me. "Once for all," I continued, "let me tell you that it is vain to tempt one whose happiness consists in giving happiness to others."

"I cannot understand you," he said ruefully. "What is to tempt?"

"Poor woodland creature!" said I, turning round. "How could you understand? It was idle of me to chide you. It is not in your little nature to comprehend a life of self-denial. Ah! if only I could reach you!"

"You have reached him," said the hill.

"If only I could touch you!"

"You have touched him," said the hill.

"But I will never leave you," burst out the Faun. "I will sweep out your shrine for you, I will accompany you to the meetings of matrons. I will enrich you at the bazaars."

I shook my head. "For these things I care not at all. And indeed I was minded to reject your offer of service together. There I was wrong. You shall help me – you shall help me to make others happy."

"Dear priest, what a curious life! People whom I have never seen – people who cannot see me – why should I make them happy?"

"My poor lad – perhaps in time you will learn why. Now begone: commence. On this very hill sits a young lady for whom I have a high regard. Commence with her. Aha! your face falls. I thought as much. You cannot do anything. Here is the conclusion of the whole matter!"

"I can make her happy," he replied, "if you order me! and when I have done so, perhaps you will trust me more."

Emily's mother had started home, but Emily and the little friend still sat beside the tea-things – she in her white pique dress and biscuit straw, he in his rough but well-cut summer suit. The great pagan figure of the Faun towered insolently above them.

The friend was saying, "And have you never felt the appalling loneliness of a crowd?"

"All that," replied Emily, "have I felt, and very much more."

Then the Faun laid his hands upon them. They, who had only intended a little cultured flirtation, resisted him as long as they could, but were gradually urged into each other's arms, and embraced with passion.

"Miscreant!" I shouted, bursting from the wood. "You have betrayed me."

"I know it: I care not," cried the little friend. "Stand aside. You are in the presence

of that which you do not understand. In the great solitude we have found ourselves at last."

"Remove your accursed hands!" I shrieked to the Faun.

He obeyed and the little friend continued more calmly: "It is idle to chide. What should you know, poor clerical creature, of the mystery of love of the eternal man and the eternal woman, of the self-effectuation of a soul?"

"That is true," said Emily angrily. "Harry, you would never have made me happy. I shall treat you as a friend, but how could I give myself to a man who makes such silly jokes? When you played the buffoon at tea, your hour was sealed. I must be treated seriously: I must see infinities broadening around me as I rise. You may not approve of it, but so I am. In the great solitude I have found myself at last."

"Wretched girl!" I cried. "Great solitude! O pair of helpless puppets –"

The little friend began to lead Emily away, but I heard her whisper to him: "Dear, we can't possibly leave the basket for Harry after this: and mother's rug; do you mind having that in the other hand?"

So they departed and I flung myself upon the ground with every appearance of despair.

"Does he cry?" said the Faun.

"He does not cry," answered the hill. "His eyes are as dry as pebbles."

My tormentor made me look at him. "I see happiness at the bottom of your heart," said he.

"I trust I have my secret springs," I answered stiffly. And then I prepared a scathing denunciation, but of all the words I might have said, I only said one and it began with "D."

He gave a joyful cry, "Oh, now you really belong to us. To the end of your life you will swear when you are cross and laugh when you are happy. Now laugh!"

There was a great silence. All nature stood waiting, while a curate tried to conceal his thoughts not only from nature but from himself. I thought of my injured pride, of my baffled unselfishness, of Emily, whom I was losing through no fault of her own, of the little friend, who just then slipped beneath the heavy tea basket, and that decided me, and I laughed.

That evening, for the first time, I heard the chalk downs singing to each other across the valleys, as they often do when the air is quiet and they have had a comfortable day. From my study window I could see the sunlit figure of the Faun, sitting before the beech copse as a man sits before his house. And as night came on I knew for certain that not only was he asleep, but that the hills and woods were asleep also. The stream, of course, never slept, any more than it ever freezes. Indeed, the hour of darkness is really the hour of water, which has been somewhat stifled all day by the great pulsings of the land. That is why you can feel it and hear it from a greater distance in the night, and why a bath after sundown is most wonderful.

The joy of that first evening is still clear in my memory, in spite of all the happy years that have followed. I remember it when I ascend my pulpit – I have a living now – and look down upon the best people sitting beneath me pew after pew, generous and contented, upon the worst people, crowded in the aisles, upon the whiskered tenors of the choir, and the high-browed curates and the church-wardens fingering their bags, and the supercilious vergers who turn latecomers from the door.

I remember it also when I sit in my comfortable bachelor rectory, amidst the carpet slippers that good young ladies I have worked for me, and the oak brackets that have been carved for me by good young men; amidst my phalanx of presentation teapots and my illuminated testimonials and all the other offerings of people who believe that I have given them a helping hand, and who really have helped me out of the mire themselves. And though I try to communicate that joy to others – as I try to communicate anything else that seems good – and though I sometimes succeed, yet I can tell no one exactly how it came to me. For if I breathed one word of that, my present life, so agreeable and profitable, would come to an end, my congregation would depart, and so should I, and instead of being an asset to my parish, I might find myself an expense to the nation. Therefore in the place of the lyrical and rhetorical treatment, so suitable to the subject, so congenial to my profession, I have been forced to use the unworthy medium of a narrative, and to delude you by declaring that this is a short story, suitable for reading in the train.

The Road from Colonus

For no very intelligible reason, Mr. Lucas had hurried ahead of his party. He was perhaps reaching the age at which independence becomes valuable, because it is so soon to be lost. Tired of attention and consideration, he liked breaking away from the younger members, to ride by himself, and to dismount unassisted. Perhaps he also relished that more subtle pleasure of being kept waiting for lunch, and of telling the others on their arrival that it was of no consequence.

So, with childish impatience, he battered the animal's sides with his heels, and made the muleteer bang it with a thick stick and prick it with a sharp one, and jolted down the hillsides through clumps of flowering shrubs and stretches of anemones and asphodel, till he heard the sound of running water, and came in sight of the group of plane trees where they were to have their meal.

Even in England those trees would have been remarkable, so huge were they, so interlaced, so magnificently clothed in quivering green. And here in Greece they were unique, the one cool spot in that hard brilliant landscape, already scorched by the heat of an April sun. In their midst was hidden a tiny Khan or country inn, a frail and mud building with a broad wooden balcony in which sat an old woman spinning, while a small brown pig, eating orange peel, stood beside her. On the wet earth below squatted two children, playing some primeval game with their fingers; and their mother, none too clean either, was messing with some rice inside. As Mrs. Forman would have said, it was all very Greek, and the fastidious Mr. Lucas felt thankful that they were bringing their own food with them, and should eat it in the open air.

Still, he was glad to be there – the muleteer had helped him off – and glad that Mrs. Forman was not there to forestall his opinions – glad even that he should not see Ethel for quite half an hour. Ethel was his youngest daughter, still unmarried. She was unselfish and affectionate, and it was generally understood that she was to devote her life to her father, and be the comfort of his old age. Mrs. Forman always referred to her as Antigone, and Mr. Lucas tried to settle down to the role of Oedipus, which seemed the only one that public opinion allowed him.

He had this in common with Oedipus, that he was growing old. Even to himself it had become obvious. He had lost interest in other people's affairs, and seldom attended when they spoke to him. He was fond of talking himself but often forgot what he was going to say, and even when he succeeded, it seldom seemed worth the effort. His phrases and gestures had become stiff and set, his anecdotes, once so successful, fell flat, his silence was as meaningless as his speech. Yet he had led a healthy, active life, had worked steadily, made money, educated his children. There was nothing and no one to blame: he was simply growing old.

At the present moment, here he was in Greece, and one of the dreams of his life was realized. Forty years ago he had caught the fever of Hellenism, and all his life he had felt that could he but visit that land, he would not have lived in vain. But Athens had been dusty, Delphi wet, Thermopylae flat, and he had listened with amazement and cynicism to the rapturous exclamations of his companions. Greece was like England: it was a man who was growing old, and it made no difference whether that man looked at the Thames or the Eurotas. It was his last hope of contradicting that logic of experience, and it was failing.

Yet Greece had done something for him, though he did not know it. It had made him discontented, and there are stirrings of life in discontent. He knew that he was not the victim of continual ill-luck. Something great was wrong, and he was pitted against no mediocre or accidental enemy. For the last month a strange desire had possessed him to die fighting.

"Greece is the land for young people," he said to himself as he stood under the plane trees, "but I will enter into it, I will possess it. Leaves shall be green again, water shall be sweet, the sky shall be blue. They were so forty years ago, and I will win them back. I do mind being old, and I will pretend no longer."

He took two steps forward, and immediately cold waters were gurgling over his ankle.

"Where does the water come from?" he asked himself. "I do not even know that." He remembered that all the hillsides were dry; yet here the road was suddenly covered with flowing streams.

He stopped still in amazement, saying: "Water out of a tree – out of a hollow tree? I never saw nor thought of that before."

For the enormous plane that leant towards the Khan was hollow – it had been burnt out for charcoal – and from its living trunk there gushed an impetuous spring, coating the bark with fern and moss, and flowing over the mule track to create fertile meadows beyond. The simple country folk had paid to beauty and mystery such tribute as they could, for in the rind of the tree a shrine was cut, holding a lamp and a little picture of the Virgin, inheritor of the Naiad's and Dryad's joint abode.

"I never saw anything so marvelous before," said Mr. Lucas. "I could even step inside the trunk and see where the water comes from."

For a moment he hesitated to violate the shrine. Then he remembered with a smile his own thought – "the place shall be mine; I will enter it and possess it" – and leapt almost aggressively onto a stone within.

The water pressed up steadily and noiselessly from the hollow roots and hidden crevices of they plane, forming a wonderful amber pool ere it spilt over the lip of bark on to the earth outside. Mr. Lucas tasted it and it was sweet, and when he looked up the black funnel of the trunk he saw sky which was blue, and some leaves which were green; and he remembered, without smiling, another of his thoughts.

Others had been before him – indeed he had a curious sense of companionship. Little votive offerings to the presiding Power were fastened on to the bark – tiny arms and legs and eyes in tin, grotesque models of the brain or the heart – all tokens of some recovery of strength or wisdom or love. There was no such thing as the solitude of nature, for the sorrows and joys of humanity had pressed even into the bosom of a tree. He spread out his arms and steadied himself against the soft charred wood, and then slowly leant back, till his body was resting on the trunk behind. His eyes closed, and he had the strange feeling of one who is moving, yet at peace – the feeling of the swimmer, who, after long struggling with chopping seas, finds that after all the tide will sweep him to his goal.

So he lay motionless, conscious only of the stream below his feet, and that all things were a stream, in which he was moving.

He was aroused at last by a shock – the shock of an arrival perhaps, for when he opened his eyes, something unimagined, indefinable, had passed over all things, and made them intelligible and good.

There was meaning in the stoop of the old woman over her work, and in the quick motions of the little pig, and in her diminishing globe of wool. A young man came singing over the streams on a mule, and there was beauty in his pose and sincerity in his greeting. The sun made no accidental patterns upon the spreading roots of the trees, and there was intention in the nodding clumps of asphodel, and in the music of the water. To Mr. Lucas, who, in a brief space of time, had discovered not only Greece, but England and all the world and life, there seemed nothing ludicrous in the desire to hang within the tree another votive offering – a little model of an entire man.

"Why, here's papa, playing at being Merlin."

All unnoticed they had arrived – Ethel, Mrs. Forman, Mr. Graham, and the English-speaking dragoman. Mr. Lucas peered out at them suspiciously. They had suddenly become unfamiliar, and all that they did seemed strained and coarse.

"Allow me to give you a hand," said Mr. Graham, a young man who was always polite to his elders.

Mr. Lucas felt annoyed. "Thank you, I can manage perfectly well by myself," he replied. His foot slipped as he stepped out of the tree, and went into the spring.

"Oh papa, my papa!" said Ethel, "what are you doing? Thank goodness I have got a change for you on the mule."

She tended him carefully, giving him clean socks and dry boots, and then sat him down on the rug beside the lunch basket, while she went with the others to explore the grove.

They came back in ecstasies, in which Mr. Lucas tried to join. But he found them intolerable. Their enthusiasm was superficial, commonplace, and spasmodic. They had no perception of the coherent beauty that was flowering around them. He tried at least to explain his feelings, and what he said was:

"I am altogether pleased with the appearance of this place. It impresses me very favorably. The trees are fine, remarkably fine for Greece, and there is something very poetic in the spring of clear running water. The people too seem kindly and civil. It is decidedly an attractive place."

Mrs. Forman upbraided him for his tepid praise.

"Oh, it is a place in a thousand!" she cried, "I could live and die here! I really would stop if I had not to be back at Athens! It reminds me of the Colonus of Sophocles."

"Well, I must stop," said Ethel. "I positively must."

"Yes, do! You and your father! Antigone and Oedipus. Of course you must stop at Colonus!"

Mr. Lucas was almost breathless with excitement. When he stood within the tree, he had believed that his happiness would be independent of locality. But these few minutes' conversation had undeceived him. He no longer trusted himself to journey through the world, for old thoughts, old wearinesses might be waiting to rejoin him as soon as he left the shade of the planes, and the music of the virgin water. To sleep in the Khan with the gracious, kind-eyed country people, to watch the bats flit about within the globe of shade, and see the moon turn the golden patterns into silver – one such night would place him beyond relapse, and confirm him forever, in the kingdom he had regained. But all his lips could say was: "I should be willing to put in a night here."

"You mean a week, papa! It would be sacrilege to put in less."

"A week then, a week," said his lips, irritated at being corrected, while his heart was leaping with joy. All through lunch he spoke to them no more, but watched the place he should know so well, and the people who would so soon be his companions and friends. The inmates of the Khan only consisted of an old woman, a middle-aged woman, a young man and two children, and to none of them had he spoken, yet he loved them as he loved everything that moved or breathed or existed beneath the benedictory shade of the planes.

"En route!" said the shrill voice of Mrs. Forman. "Ethel! Mr. Graham! The best of things must end."

"Tonight," thought Mr. Lucas, "they will light the little lamp by the shrine. And when we all sit together on the balcony, perhaps they will tell me which offerings they put up."

"I beg your pardon, Mr. Lucas," said Graham, "but they want to fold up the rug you are sitting on."

Mr. Lucas got up, saying to himself: "Ethel shall go to bed first, and then I will try to tell them about my offering too – for it is a thing I must do. I think they will understand if I am left with them alone."

Ethel touched him on the cheek. "Papa! I've called you three times. All the mules are here."

"Mules? What mules?"

"Our mules. We're all waiting. Oh, Mr. Graham, do help my father on."

"I don't know what you're talking about, Ethel."

"My dearest papa, we must start. You know we have to get to Olympia tonight."

Mr. Lucas in pompous, confident tones replied: "I always did wish, Ethel, that you had a better head for plans. You know perfectly well that we are putting in a week here. It is your own suggestion."

Ethel was startled into impoliteness. "What a perfectly ridiculous idea. You must have known I was joking. Of course I meant I wished we could."

"Ah! if we could only do what we wished!" sighed Mrs. Forman, already seated on her mule.

"Surely," Ethel continued in calmer tones, "you didn't think I meant it."

"Most certainly I did. I have made all my plans on the supposition that we are stopping here, and it will be extremely inconvenient, indeed, impossible for me to start."

He delivered this remark with an air of great conviction, and Mrs. Forman and Mr. Graham had to turn away to hide their smiles

"I am sorry I spoke so carelessly; it was wrong of me. But, you know, we can't break up our party, and even one night here would make us miss the boat at Patras."

Mrs. Forman, in an aside, called Mr. Graham's attention to the excellent way in which Ethel managed her father.

"I don't mind about the Patras boat. You said that we should stop here, and we are stopping."

It seemed as if the inhabitants of the Khan had divined in some mysterious way that the altercation touched them. The old woman stopped her spinning, while the young man and the two children stood behind Mr. Lucas, as if supporting him.

Neither arguments nor entreaties moved him. He said little, but he was absolutely determined, because for the first time he saw his daily life aright. What need had he to return to England? Who would miss him? His friends were dead or cold. Ethel loved him in a way, but, as was right, she had other interests. His other children he seldom saw. He had only one other relative, his sister Julia, whom he both feared and hated. It was no effort to struggle. He would be a fool as well as a coward if he stirred from the place which brought him happiness and peace.

At last Ethel, to humor him, and not disinclined to air her modern Greek, went into the Khan with the astonished dragoman to look at the rooms. The woman inside received them with loud welcomes, and the young man, when no one was looking, began to lead Mr. Lucas' mule to the stable.

"Drop it, you brigand!" shouted Graham, who always declared that foreigners could understand English if they chose. He was right, for the man obeyed, and they all stood waiting for Ethel's return.

She emerged at last, with close-gathered skirts, followed by the dragoman bearing the little pig, which he had bought at a bargain.

"My dear papa, I will do all I can for you, but stop in that Khan – no."

"Are there – fleas?" asked Mrs. Forman.

Ethel intimated that "fleas" was not the word.

"Well, I am afraid that settles it," said Mrs. Forman, "I know how particular Mr. Lucas is."

"It does not settle it," said Mr. Lucas. "Ethel, you go on. I do not want you. I don't know why I ever consulted you. I shall stop here alone."

"That is absolute nonsense," said Ethel, losing her temper. "How can you be left alone at your age? How would you get your meals or your bath? All your letters are waiting for you at Patras. You'll miss the boat. That means missing the London operas, and upsetting all your engagements for the month. And as if you could travel by yourself!"

"They might knife you," was Mr. Graham's contribution.

The Greeks said nothing; but whenever Mr. Lucas looked their way, they beckoned him towards the Khan. The children would even have drawn him by the coat, and the old woman on the balcony stopped her almost completed spinning, and fixed him with mysterious appealing eyes. As he fought, the issue assumed gigantic proportions, and he believed that he was not merely stopping because he had regained youth or seen beauty or found happiness, but because in that place and with those people a supreme event was awaiting him which would transfigure the face of the world. The moment was so tremendous that he abandoned words and arguments as useless, and rested on the strength of his mighty unrevealed allies: silent men, murmuring water, and whispering trees. For the whole place called with one voice, articulate to him, and his garrulous opponents became every minute more meaningless and absurd. Soon they would be tired and go chattering away into the sun, leaving him to the cool grove and the moonlight and the destiny he foresaw.

Mrs. Forman and the dragoman had indeed already started, amid the piercing screams of the little pig, and the struggle might have gone on indefinitely if Ethel had not called in Mr. Graham.

"Can you help me?" she whispered. "He is absolutely unmanageable."

"I'm no good at arguing – but if I could help you in any other way –" and he looked down complacently at his well-made figure.

Ethel hesitated. Then she said: "Help me in any way you can. After all, it is for his good that we do it."

"Then have his mule led up behind him."

So when Mr. Lucas thought he had gained the day, he suddenly felt himself lifted off the ground, and set sideways on the saddle, and at the same time the mule started off at a trot. He said nothing, for he had nothing to say, and even his face showed little emotion as he felt the shade pass and heard the sound of the water cease. Mr. Graham was running at his side, hat in hand, apologizing.

"I know I had no business to do it, and I do beg your pardon awfully. But I do hope that someday you too will feel that I was – damn!"

A stone had caught him in the middle of the back. It was thrown by the little boy, who was pursuing them along the mule track. He was followed by his sister, also throwing stones.

Ethel screamed to the dragoman, who was some way ahead with Mrs. Forman, but before he could rejoin them, another adversary appeared. It was the young Greek, who had cut them off in front, and now dashed down at Mr. Lucas' bridle. Fortunately Graham was an expert boxer, and it did not take him a moment to beat down the youth's feeble defense, and to send him sprawling with a bleeding mouth into the asphodel. By this time the dragoman bad arrived, the children, alarmed at the fate of their brother, had desisted, and the rescue party, if such it is to be considered, retired in disorder to the trees.

"Little devils!" said Graham, laughing with triumph. "That's the modern Greek all over. Your father meant money if he stopped, and they consider we were taking it out of their pocket."

"Oh, they are terrible – simple savages! I don't know how I shall ever thank you. You've saved my father."

"I only hope you didn't think me brutal"

"No," replied Ethel with a little sigh. "I admire strength."

Meanwhile the cavalcade reformed, and Mr. Lucas, who, as Mrs. Forman said, bore his disappointment wonderfully well, was put comfortably on to his mule. They hurried up the opposite hillside, fearful of another attack, and it was not until they had left the eventful place far behind that Ethel found an opportunity to speak to her father and ask his pardon for the way she had treated him.

"You seemed so different, dear father, and you quite frightened me. Now I feel that you are your old self again."

He did not answer, and she concluded that he was not unnaturally offended at her behavior.

By one of those curious tricks of mountain scenery, the place they had left an hour before suddenly reappeared far below them. The Khan was hidden under the green dome, but in the open there still stood three figures, and through the pure air rose up a faint cry of defiance or farewell.

Mr. Lucas stopped irresolutely, and let the reins fall from his hand.

"Come, father dear," said Ethel gently.

He obeyed, and in another moment a spur of the hill hid the dangerous scene forever.

II.

It was breakfast time, but the gas was alight, owing to the fog. Mr. Lucas was in the middle of an account of a bad night he had spent. Ethel, who was to be married in a few weeks, had her arms on the table, listening.

"First the door bell rang, then you came back from the theater. Then the dog started, and after the dog the cat. And at three in the morning a young hooligan passed by singing. Oh yes: then there was the water gurgling in the pipe above my head."

"I think that was only the bath water running away," said Ethel, looking rather worn.

"Well, there's nothing I dislike more than running water. It's perfectly impossible to sleep in the house. I shall give it up. I shall give notice next quarter. I shall tell the landlord plainly, 'The reason I am giving up the house is this: it is perfectly impossible to sleep in it.' If he says – says – well, what has he got to say?"

"Some more toast, father?"

"Thank you, my dear." He took it, and there was an interval of peace.

But he soon recommenced. "I'm not going to submit to the practicing next door as tamely as they think. I wrote and told there so – didn't I?"

"'Yes," said Ethel, who had taken care that the letter should not reach. "I have seen the governess, and she has promised to arrange it differently. And Aunt Julia hates noise. It will be sure to be all right."

Her aunt, being the only unattached member of the family, was coming to keep house for her father when she left him. The reference was not a happy one, and Mr. Lucas commenced a series of half articulate sighs, which was only stopped by the arrival of the post.

"Oh, what a parcel!" cried Ethel. "For me! What can it be! Greek stamps. This is most exciting!"

It proved to be some asphodel bulbs, sent by Mrs. Forman from Athens for planting in the conservatory.

"Doesn't it bring it all back! You remember the asphodels, father. And all wrapped up in Greek newspapers. I wonder if I can read them still, I used to be able to, you know."

She rattled on, hoping to conceal the laughter of the children next door – a favorite source of querulousness at breakfast time.

"Listen to me! 'A rural disaster.' Oh, I've hit on something sad. But never mind. 'Last Tuesday at Plataniste, in the province of Messenia, a shocking tragedy occurred. A large tree' – aren't I getting on well? – 'blew down in the night and' – wait a minute – oh, dear!' crushed to death the five occupants of the little Khan there, who had apparently been sitting in the balcony. The bodies of Maria Rhomaides, the aged proprietress, and of her daughter, aged forty-six, were easily recognizable, whereas that of her grandson' – oh, the rest is really too horrid; I wish I had never tried it, and what's more I feel to have heard the name Plataniste before. We didn't stop there, did we, in the spring?"

"We had lunch," said Mr. Lucas, with a faint expression of trouble on his vacant face. "Perhaps it was where the dragoman bought the pig."

"Of course," said Ethel in a nervous voice. "Where the dragoman bought the little pig. How terrible!"

"Very terrible!" said her father, whose attention was wandering to the noisy children next door. Ethel suddenly started to her feet with genuine interest.

"Good gracious!" she exclaimed. "This is an old paper. It happened not lately but in April – the night of Tuesday the eighteenth – and we – we must have been there in the afternoon."

"So we were," said Mr. Lucas. She put her hand to her heart, scarcely able to speak.

"Father, dear father, I must say it: you wanted to stop there. All those people, those poor half savage people, tried to keep you, they're dead. The whole place, it says, is in ruins, and even the stream has changed its course. Father, dear, if it had not been for me, and if Arthur had not helped me, you must have been killed."

Mr. Lucas waved his hand irritably. "It is not a bit of good speaking to the governess, I shall write to the landlord and say, 'The reason I am giving up the house is this: the dog barks, the children next door are intolerable, and I cannot stand the noise of running water.'"

Ethel did not check his babbling. She was aghast at the narrowness of the escape, and for a long time kept silence. At last she said: "Such a marvelous deliverance does make one believe in Providence."

Mr. Lucas, who was still composing his letter to the landlord, did not reply.

39342541R00051

Printed in Poland
by Amazon Fulfillment
Poland Sp. z o.o., Wrocław